To my Work Big Bro —
   Thanks for supporting my dream,
being an amazing teaching partner, and
an incredibly loyal friend!
      Thanks again, Jason ☺

TURN

EMILY
VAN ENGEN

Emily Van Engen

[Work Sis]

Published by Emily Van Engen
www.emilyvanengen.com

Cover images by Paper & Sage Design

Developmental Editing by D Tinker Editing
Copyediting and Formatting by L.A. Boles

ISBN-13: 978-0692186138
ISBN-10: 0692186131

To my brown-eyed boys

I

Monday, September 5, 2016

Something is wrong.

My feet and legs feel like lead, glued to the floor. The sound of my pounding heart echoes through my ribcage, I'm convinced it is audible. My chest grows tight with anxiety.

My vision was blinded with light but now darkness consumes the spaces around me. My eyes struggle to adjust. Blinking doesn't seem to help so I stare into the void, waiting for relief.

After an agonizing amount of time passes, I begin to see orange beams escape from the slits of a double window on the far wall. The rays of light are active with dust. The light is uneven and shines through one side of the set of windows. Its source is far and gives little visibility to my surroundings. It flickers like moths around a street lamp.

With the slight visibility I've gained, I take a deep breath. A moldy smell invades my nostrils and makes my stomach sour. The ache from my empty abdomen causes my eyes to squeeze with pain. It feels like I haven't eaten in years.

Where am I? How did I get here?

I try to think back to the last place I was when it dawns on me...I don't even know who I am.

I can't remember anything.

I should try to run, find help, but my breathing is shallow, my heart is racing, and I'm lightheaded. Fear consumes me, but I decide not to let it defeat me.

As I continue through the stages of my panic attack, I look down to assess. With what little visibility I have, I can see that my hands and feet are not bound, but free. No cuts, bruises, or signs of a struggle. I try to take a few steps, but fear has rendered my legs frozen.

If I make noise, someone might hear me, though I'm not sure who that someone would be.

I look toward the far side of the room and can see couches covered in sheets. I'm in a large space, maybe a living room. About an inch of dust blankets the end tables and coffee table. Unfortunately, the portion of the room in front of me remains dark despite the light illumination of the furniture.

Whoever brought me here, did so on purpose. Why else put me in a place so obviously abandoned? But why not tie me up? Why not be here when I woke up?

Fear shoots down my spine, causing a wave of prickling across the back of my neck. My breath quickens and my palms grow sweaty.

Despite the stench, I breathe deep and exhale slow to grasp rationality. I take off my glasses and wipe my eyes, hoping when my vision adjusts that I'll remember my life or be somewhere warm and familiar. Instead, this bleak place comes back into view and anger replaces my fear. What happened to make me forget everything?

I may not know who I am, but I know I'm not a coward.

My sudden boldness lightens my steps. I move forward at normal speed, my right hand flat on the wall as a balance. As my steps grow confident, my shin sends an object shattering to the floor. My breath catches in my throat and my body halts. From the weight and size, I'd say it was a vase but in the dark, I can't be sure.

I try to recover from the jolt of the container, but my heart races in my chest. Stepping over the wreckage, I continue toward what could be a door but my hand slams into something on the wall, a shattering sound follows.

"SERIOUSLY?" The word shoots out of my mouth and my hands smack tight around my lips and chin. I shut my eyes tight, waiting for them to come.

After what seems like eternity, I realize no one is coming. I crack my knuckles and shake out my hands. I'm ready to get out of here. Just as I'm about to keep moving, something catches my eye. A strange glow radiates out of the periphery of my left eye. I turn my head to see what it is…

WHAM!

The door in front of me flings open and a cool breeze and blinding light flood into the dusty room. A shadow of a person enters and screams, "Get on your knees and put your hands where I can see them!"

Before I can process what's happening, I am slammed to the floor…

Tuesday, September 5, 2017

"Are you okay?"

I open my eyes and look around. I'm wrapped up in my sheets and blankets on the cold floor of the boy's sleeping quarters with Renner staring at me like I wet myself. I look down to make sure I haven't.

Safe from ridicule this time.

"I'm fine." I pull myself up off the floor and unwrap the sheets from around my waist.

Renner laughs as he puts his jacket on, zipping it up midway. "It's a good thing I let you have the bottom bunk. If you fell from the top, yikes." He shakes his head. "Which nightmare this time?"

I sit on the edge of the bed with my arms resting on my thighs, my breathing still shallow. "The night they found me."

Renner stops tying his combat boot and looks up at me. "Oh man. That sucks." He furrows his brow, looking unsure of what to say, and goes back to tying.

"It's been a year. I knew it was coming up but..." I put my head in my hands and it feels heavier than usual.

Renner stands up, his eyebrows follow suit. "I hope you weren't expecting an anniversary card."

Sarcasm fills the air around us. I decide to add to it. "Oh hey, your birthday card is back at the store if you want to know what I picked out for you. Sincerely, seventeen is trivial age in the grand scheme of life..."

My bunkmate whacks me on the side of the head with my own pillow. A smile breaks on the right corner of his mouth.

"Go shower, nerd. You stink and it's the first day of school." He tosses the pillow into my abdomen and leaves, heading for the dining room.

I grab my shower caddy and head for the boy's bathroom, but I stop and lean up against one of the six metal bunk beds, with their identical sheets and pillows. The sun refracts through the sheer, white curtains on the front window.

Despite the light, I live in darkness. How is it I still have no memories from before that night?

🕐🕑🕒🕓🕔

"I don't think you want to remember." Renner laughs as we walk out the front door of the children's home.

"You know I do! I can't believe you're joking about this."

"Oh, come on Damon! If anyone is going to joke with you about this, it's me." He nudges me in jest. "Oh shoot, hold on. I forgot something."

Renner goes back towards the house, smacking the "Pilut Home for Children" sign on his way up the sidewalk. Heaving from the quick jog in and out, he pulls his backpack off and sets it on the ground. He concentrates on putting his beat up, stained copy of *Walden; or Life in the Woods* by Henry David Thoreau inside and rezips the bag secure and we resume our trek to school.

"Sorry about that."

"It's okay. I get it." And I do.

I'd give anything to have *something* from my family.

"Are you going to come by the archery range after school today?" Renner's voice rises as a begging smile sweeps his face.

I shake my head. "I have my appointment with Dr. Habibah."

We reach the grounds of Nomad High School. The sign glitters in purple and gold, with script lettering: "Home of the Fighting Camels." Living in this part of the country, one might expect this sort of corny mascot. I suppose it could be worse. We could be boats or unicorns.

Despite the strange name, Nomad isn't the worst place to live. It's a typical Midwestern village of about 3,000 people. Small, but big enough that that we have stoplights and chain restaurants. I ended up in Nomad because it had the closest children's home with an empty bed. Dr. Habibah, my psychologist, thought going to high school with regular teenagers might help bring up memories of my past.

It hasn't. If anything, it has kept me isolated. High school is tough and anyone who tries to say different is lying.

We walk through the glass double doors and enter what's known as "the commons," where social factions interact before the warning bell. I walk past the factions, trying to keep my head up. The archery club absorbs Renner the way a meteor gets pulled into a planet's atmosphere. On the far side, athletes high-five and discuss their summer filled with the madness of travel sports. Closer to the offices, the academics compare class schedules. Under the stairs, the gamers brag about their many wins in their online conquests while the slackers hide in a dark corner, doing who-knows-what. The gossip network occupies the entire center of the commons, whispering and laughing. At the center of the chatter is blabbermouth extraordinaire, Hannah. Lucky for me, no one from that clan stops to consider me as I focus my steps toward the library.

The first day I attended Nomad High, students from all cliques stared at me and muttered under their breath. When I walked down the hall, students dodged my path to avoid me. For them, it was easier to ignore the strange and uncomfortable rather than learning about it. I appreciate the school preaching inclusion but the truth is, if you don't fit in with any of the social factions, you're doomed to be an outsider.

That's why I spend my mornings in the library.

The first bell of the day rings but I'm so engrossed in a book, I ignore it. I feel a pinch to the back of my neck and I jump.

"Calm down. It's just me."

I close my eyes and breathe deep. Renner picks up my book.

"This one, again?"

I snatch the book from his hand and put it back on the shelf. "*Time Travel: A Study in Human Capability* by Dr. Ivan Navi is the leading resource on chronological boundaries and exploration."

"I'm going to be honest, I didn't understand a word you just said."

"Should I be surprised?"

Renner punches me on the arm as the warning bell rings. "Let's go. We're going to be late for Bard's class."

Even though I'm just a junior, I'll be in the same senior Intro to Molecular Biology class as Renner. Mr. Bard, the head of the science department, figured out after two days in his class last year that I have a high aptitude for science. I tested out of earth science, biology, chemistry, and physics. He scheduled me in his first hour this year because he felt that as a sixteen-year-old, I wasn't being challenged enough, at least not scientifically.

Today's class is spent going over the syllabus and class procedures. When the bell rings, Renner stands up and puts out a fist. "I'm going to my locker. I'll see you at dinner."

I give him a fist bump and we go our separate ways.

🕐🕑🕒🕓🕔

"So how are you feeling today, Damon?" Dr. Habibah pulls out her notebook and pen. We meet at the hospital in Nomad since it's walking distance from school and the home, and it's only an hour and a half drive from Trevoc Hospital once a week.

"I'm pretty tired today." To be honest, I'm quite aggravated. Dr. Habibah was the on-call psychologist the night I was found. After hours of accusations of breaking and entering and vandalism, the police transferred me to Dr. Habibah's care at the hospital. She diagnosed me with dissociative amnesia. I want to remember my life and who I am, but my brain is blocking it out. I've been meeting with her every week since that night, but I still can't remember anything.

"Nervous about your first day of junior year?"

"Hardly." I look down at my hands and trace the lines of my right palm. "I had another nightmare last night."

She puts her reading glasses on the end of her nose and scribbles in her pad. She glances back up at me with her henna colored eyes and waits for me to initiate, which always annoys.

"The night they found me in Trevoc."

"I was wondering if your subconscious would remember."

"Apparently." I'm terse. I sit up in my chair and straighten my glasses. "Dr. Habibah, why is it after a year of sessions, I'm still no closer to figuring out who I am or what happened to me?" I'm trying to keep my frustration levels low but I'm not doing a very good job at it.

She removes her glasses and relaxes her body. Her calm demeanor is especially irritating today. "Damon, I promise, your memories are in there. They are blocked because your traumatic abduct—"

"But don't you think if I was abducted, there would be a missing person's report from someone in my family? No one went looking for me and it would be improbable that my entire family is dead."

Dr. Habibah puts her glasses back on and writes a few things in her notebook. Her long black hair is starting to grey at the roots, though she can't be older than early forties. She's always been kind to me and I'm grateful for that. I don't, however, think she's very helpful in trying to restore my memories. She focuses on the day-to-day and how I'm adjusting to my life in Nomad. My life without memories.

"Damon, let's focus on today for now." Like magic, she reads my mind. "How was your first day of school?"

When Dr. Habibah avoids the hard questions regarding my apparent abduction, it makes me irritable. I know she cares and has her own pace of therapy, but this branch of science doesn't interest me. Despite my impatience, I like the consistency of her appointments. "I still don't feel like I really fit in here. When you go to school with a possible abduction victim who doesn't remember his life, kids tend to stay away from you."

"You have Renner."

I don't want to admit it, but she's right. After a week of police interrogations and seemingly endless medical testing, they brought me to the children's home where Renner offered me the bottom bunk. Ever since then, we've been friends. Renner became my support system on the spot. He didn't even know me. He still doesn't really know me. I guess we have that in common.

"It's hard when I feel like there is more to my story but no one knows what it is. Not even me—"

Dr. Habibah's cell phone interrupts my thoughts. She looks at the screen and holds a finger to me. "It's my assistant. He only calls in emergencies. I'll just be a second...Hello?

...You know I'm in a session in Nomad right now...

...wait slow down...

...where...where was she found..."

Dr. Habibah stiffens, her eyes fixed on mine. The color drains from her face and seems like she could break into a sweat any second. "Okay. I'm on my way right now. Don't let anyone else talk to her until I get there." She hangs up the phone and stuffs it into her purse. She gathers her things with haste and I cough to catch her attention.

"Oh, I'm so sorry Damon. I hate to cut our session short but there's an emergency back in Trevoc and it is urgent that I return."

What?

"Okay. I'll see you next week then?"

"Um—" Dr. Habibah stumbles over her words. "I'm going to have to get back to you about our next session. This new case may take a bit to sort out."

"Okay, well good luck..." The door slams behind her. If this were a cartoon, she'd have a smoke trail like the Road Runner for the speed at which she escaped.

I hope my frustration didn't cause her to leave faster.

II

I decide, since my session was cut short by fifty-five minutes, to walk over to the archery field to meet up with Renner. The range is in the farthest corner of the town, but the walk isn't too bad from the hospital. A small dirt path veers from the sidewalk into the woods. Large Oak trees thicken the forest with their widespread branches. A breeze keeps the air from being too humid, but the clouds above loom. The cumulus clouds billow upward and are darkening. Even though the sun beams peaking between the clouds make the sky look serene, I can almost guarantee we're getting hit with a storm tonight.

I watch Renner from the edge of the field. By himself as usual, he nocks an arrow, aims, and releases, striking the straw outside of the target.

"You know I hate it when you lurk like that." Renner voices loud enough for me to hear.

"I thought you'd be happy to see me." He turns toward me and gives me a look of irritation. I chuckle and hike up toward the seating area of straw bales.

If Renner Emit wasn't my friend, I'd think his stature daunting. Tall and husky, constantly outfitted in dark jeans, combat boots, and a green khaki jacket zipped up to his neck. I can see how his look might be a bit intimidating to others. Maybe at this point, he wants people to avoid him.

"Dr. Habibah got an urgent phone call and had to leave our session right away."

"Bummer." Renner examines his arrow. "I'm trying to practice for nationals. Next time you plan on lurking, announce yourself so I don't waste another shot." He switches the arrow with a different one from his quiver and prepares to load up. He adjusts the gloves on his large hands. His unkempt, mane of dust colored hair flops in the breeze as he lines up his shot, dark eyes in concentration. This time, his arrow strikes the pinhole. He walks to the target and yanks his arrow out.

I don't know much about archery but according to physics, his use of force and trajectory demonstrates he's good. No. Excellent. Renner is very intelligent, but he doesn't show that to many people. Most people around town assume he's a punk kid with an agenda.

I think he's lonely.

Growing up in a children's home isn't easy. Due to his traumatic circumstances, he retreated into himself. When possible, adoptive parents came, Renner showed them his book and talked about how his parents were going to come back for him someday. This, of course, deterred families from choosing him and at a certain point, Renner aged out of adoption all together. The older he gets, the more secluded from others he becomes. It's a miracle he let me in so easily.

Renner puts the arrow in his quiver, throwing the strap over his shoulder. "Let's get home for dinner. I heard Miss Elle say this morning she was making conies, fries, and fudge."

"Wait, before we go, I have some ideas on how to improve your mechanics."

🕐🕑🕒🕓🕔

Renner and I approach the home as the sun is setting. The two-story farmhouse is old but useful. The inside was renovated back in the 1980's to better accommodate multiple children. The outside looks as tired and winter worn as any other farmhouse in the village. The wrap-around porch is most redeemable quality about the home, 360-degree views of the village stocked with rocking chairs and chain swings.

We walk in the front door and turn right into the boy's quarters to drop our backpacks off at our bunk. It's evident this room used to be a living room from the crown molding on the ceiling. There are two doors to this room, one near the front door and one at the back near the boy's bathroom. I've never been upstairs, but I know the girls sleep in the finished attic and have their own bathroom with a tub so Miss Elle can bathe the babies. I'm certain Miss Elle's bedroom is above the boy's bedroom. I often fall asleep to the freight-train sounds of her snoring.

The dining room is complete chaos when we walk in. The home is almost at full capacity with 17 children total, 6 girls and 11 boys. The littles are finishing their meals with Miss Elle. Middles, aged 10 to 13, are paired with a little to help at breakfast and dinner. Teens, 14 and older, are expected to serve and clean up after themselves. Renner taught me the dining routine when I first started living here. He explained that it helps Miss Elle since she is the sole caretaker of the Pilut Home for Children and can only do so many things at once.

Miss Elle has a tight schedule for meals, baths, and bedtime. She is strict, but not mean. In fact, she's one of the kindest people I've met since coming here. She cares for all the kids at the home, no matter how short or long their stay is.

Widowed in her late thirties with no children of her own, she committed her life to finding good homes for orphaned children. She's in her seventies now. It's amazing to see her dedication.

"Renner and Damon, you are late," Miss Elle spat as she walked through the dining room toward the kitchen. Renner grabs the short, plump woman by the arm before she can get through the door and brings her in for a big hug. She pulls down his collar, causing him to come eye to eye with her and she gives him a big kiss, planting her bright red lipstick on his cheek.

"We got held up because Damon was explaining how physics works in archery but when he tried to show me, it was a huge fail."

I exaggerate an eye roll.

"I thought you were meeting with Dr. Habibah, Damon." She examines me through her thick glasses. Her powder white Afro bounces as she taps her foot in impatience.

"I went, I promise! She had to cut the session short for some emergency back in Trevoc."

Miss Elle softens her face into a beautiful smile. For an elderly woman, you can tell she could've been a model when she was younger. She winks at me and goes back into the kitchen.

Renner and I push through the kitchen door and almost run into Miss Elle who's holding a cake with lit candles. Streamers drape the cabinets, balloons float around the ceiling. She sings a short rendition of the birthday song and Renner blows out the candles. I open a cabinet and grab the card I hid in the crockpot.

"Dude." The birthday boy shakes his head in embarrassment.

"I like to hide things. Sue me!"

A smile invades Renner's face. "Thanks."

"I know you don't like the attention, but Miss Elle told me everyone should feel special on their birthday so we planned a low-key surprise."

Miss Elle puts the cake on the counter and tells us to go out to the dining room. She's bringing us our plates as a special birthday treat.

We finish our delicious meal and I take our dishes into the kitchen to the see little Viv climbing up a stool she brought to the counter.

"Viv, what are you doing?" I lift her by her little armpits to the top of the stool.

From the other room Miss Elle yells. "Viv, I already told you! You cannot have another piece of birthday cake! You'll rot your teeth right out of your face!"

Viv hangs her head in shame; her long, blonde hair covers her face. She starts to climb down but I stop her. "Viv, I don't want my cake for dessert tonight but I also don't want Miss Elle's fine baking to go to waste. Will you eat mine?"

At lightning speed, her face pops out from beneath her curly locks, emerald eyes wide with excitement. "Yes please! Thank you, Damon!" I return her to the floor, cut my piece of cake out of the pan, and hand it to her. She hugs me tight around the knees and goes running upstairs.

Renner shakes his head in disappointment from the doorway of the kitchen.

"Come on man, she's only six. Her teeth are supposed to fall out anyway!" I grab a plate and hand it to Renner. He cracks a smile at the corner of his mouth and steps up for his own slice of cake.

🕐🕑🕓🕕🕖

Tonight, Miss Elle has a special treat for the first day of school: story time. To most kids my age, that would sound lame, but Miss Elle is the best storyteller. All the kids gather in what we call the "couch room" where the tiny television and computer are and as the name suggests, many couches. She sits in the glider, rocking the youngest baby to sleep, and asks us what she should read tonight.

Viv jumps up from the floor in her little Disney nightgown. Her clean, still wet hair whipping the people next to her as she hops up and down with her hand in the air.

"Okay, Viv. What do you want tonight?" Miss Elle sighs and chuckles with expert patience.

Viv stands frozen for a moment as she tries to remember what she was going to say after getting so excited. "Oh…I thought because it's Renner's birthday that you could read from his golden book!"

The audience turns to face Renner and his eyes widen with surprise.

"Would that be all right, Renner?" Miss Elle's voice is subdued. Her hesitancy is understandable considering how personal that book is to him.

Viv turns to face Renner, her green eyes glowing with hope. She bounds over the others and jumps into his lap. She whispers into his ear, though it's loud enough for all to hear. "Please," she whined. "It's such a pretty book. I bet it has pretty words too."

"Okay, Viv. Just for you." Viv squeals and wraps her arms around Renner in a tight squeeze. He returns the hug until her laughs become faint from the lack of oxygen. She jumps down and joins the littles near Miss Elle while Renner walks to the boy's quarters.

Besides Miss Elle and me, Viv is the only other resident at the home who isn't afraid of Renner. She arrived at the home as a newborn when Renner was eleven. Renner doesn't take to many people, at least not right away, but I think because of how helpless she was, Viv had him wrapped around her finger from the second he held her. Miss Elle said for years that Viv wouldn't go to anyone but Renner. It's rather endearing.

He comes back and hands the worn book to Miss Elle. The

pages shine golden from the edges, though spotted and stained with a mystery of fluids. The dust cover is ripped and missing pieces. It may even be stuck to the cover of the book. "Is there anything specific you recommend, Renner?"

"Go to the bookmark. My favorite passage is starred." Renner says with slight reluctance. He zips his jacket high so the collar sits right along his jaw line.

Miss Elle opens the book, uses the ribbon to find Renner's passage, and reads,

> *"I learned this, at least, by my experiment: that if one advances confidently in the direction of his dreams, and endeavors to live the life which he has imagined, he will meet with a success unexpected in common hours. He will put some things behind, will pass an invisible boundary; new, universal, and more liberal laws will begin to establish themselves around and within him; or the old laws be expanded, and interpreted in his favor in a more liberal sense, and he will live with the license of a higher order of beings. In proportion as he simplifies his life, the laws of the universe will appear less complex, and solitude will not be solitude, nor poverty poverty, nor weakness weakness. If you have built castles in the air, your work need not be lost; that is where they should be. Now put the foundations under them…"*

Startling the silent room, Renner jumps off the couch, snatches the book out of Miss Elle's hands, and leaves. Miss Elle stands up in shock, but consoles the crying baby in her arms. Streams of tears fall down Viv's face, her pitiful sniffle noises drowned out by the others. The littles whine with fear. The middles gasp to catch their breath. The teens shake their head in disappointment, letting the kitchen door slam behind them as they leave.

I make a quick exit and stop Renner at our bunk. "You scared everyone in there."

Renner balls up his hands and looks at me with a combination of pain and rage.

I put a hand on his shoulder. "I know that was hard for you—"

"No. You don't." He drops his shoulder so my hand flops back to my side. He huffs and climbs into his bed, facing the wall.

I stare at the back of his head, wondering what to do or say.

Happy Birthday, Renner.

A thunderclap shakes the house. I wish I could predict people the way I can the weather.

III

Wednesday, September 6, 2017

I woke up early this morning to see if Renner was okay, but he isn't in bed. He's probably at the archery range. I don't blame him.

The home sits quiet at this hour. Instead of going back to sleep, I decide to take advantage of the extra silence to get ready for school.

In the bathroom, I set my shower caddy down next to the first stall. I undress and wrap my waist in a fluffy towel from the shelf, in case one of the littles walks in.

I walk over to the mirror to make sure there aren't any stray zits, sleep dust, or something else I need to take care of before showering. When my eyes meet the eyes staring back at me, something strange happens. My vision flickers as if the lights were cutting in and out. I shut my eyes and shake my head. I open them again and the strobe-like flashes repeat. I rub my eyes hard this time. I look up at the light in the bathroom for a few seconds to make sure we aren't having power surges.

Nothing happens.

I drop my head so I'm looking down at my hairy toes, my hands holding each side of the porcelain sink. The flashing gave me a bit of a headache. I lift my head until my gaze is locked with the reflection in the mirror. Crystal blue eyes, similar my own, stare back at me, except they are different.

Wise.

I realize as I stare into these eyes, I'm looking up instead of straight ahead. The body in front of me is not skinny or lanky but broad with hints of muscular tone. I lift my left hand to touch my body, and the stranger in the mirror follows suit, except their hand has a gold band on the fourth finger. Contrary to my own, the wide hands are clean with well-groomed tips. I feel up to my flat neck where a prominent Adam's apple protrudes from the neck of my reflection. I set my hand back down on the sink and lean in to take a closer look at the jawline. The scruff of 5 o'clock shadow moves as I tilt and turn, even though the changes of puberty haven't quite gotten me that far yet. I notice the larger nose and ears and how the hair is a darker chestnut. It's parted on the side and styled, instead of a messy mop like mine.

The eyes meet again. This time they look scared. Desperate almost.

The person in the mirror and I take our glasses off, mine thick and brown, but his half-rimmed and black, and with a trembling hand, put them on the shelf. We reach for the sink and turn it on, careful not to lose eye contact. We fill up our hands with water.

I splash the cold in my face. I take two more handfuls and scrub hard before looking up. This time, the face that stares back is my own.

I bring my small hands to my face, and slide them down the front, rubbing hard. I shake my head at the teen in the mirror. Nightmares are one thing. Day visions, or whatever this was, are completely unacceptable.

Am I delusional?

Is this what a mental breakdown looks like?

I need to call Dr. Habibah.

Something is seriously wrong if I look in a mirror and see a grown man.

What's worse, I think it was someone I know.

Or scarier yet, someone I once knew.

🕐🕑🕒🕓🕔

M r. Bard assigns our seats in alphabetical order so he can remember our names. Since I don't know my real name and no one can figure out who I am or where I came from, the police labeled me "John Doe." I refused to answer to that name because I associate it with the unidentified dead bodies on those crime TV shows. Dr. Habibah said it would be better if I choose my own name so they asked me what I would like to be called. Stumped, I looked around the police station and noticed a tourist pamphlet for the village of Nomad hanging upside down on the wall. I told the officer, "Damon Doe" and he said that would be fine.

Since I kept my generic last name, Renner and I are next to each other. There are an odd number of people in front of us on the roster so an aisle divides us from being lab partners.

Renner writes on a piece of paper and slides it across the floor to me. *Did you ever get ahold of Dr. Habibah?*

I look at him and shake my head. He scratches his head and taps his fingers on the desk in inquiry. I respond, *I did leave her a message.* And kick it back across the tile.

Renner sighs, breaking the silence of morning bell work. He gives an awkward smile to the students who are now staring at him. He leans over his paper and looks up at the bell work question on the screen, "Name the kingdoms of the five-kingdom classification system (you should've learned this in regular biology)."

I watch him write the words animal, plant, and fungi but stops. He looks up at the ceiling tiles and scrunches his face together as if deep in thought. He turns his head to see if the class is still staring at him, but they focus on other things now.

He writes back to me. *Maybe you should pay her a visit at her hospital today. Your vision this morning should not be ignored, especially if you are turning into a psychopath.*

I give Renner an annoyed look, but he just chuckles under his breath. Before I can even realize, Mr. Bard is grabbing our note off my desk and takes it to his front counter. While opening and refolding the note, he says, "Mr. Doe and Mr. Emit, if you are going to pass notes in my class, they'd better be scientific or at least aerodynamic," and throws his perfectly creased paper airplane toward my head. The tip sticks into my crazy mop hair and I grab it and crumble it up.

The class laughs and Mr. Bard continues by going over the answers to this morning's bell work question.

While that was one of the funniest things I've ever seen a teacher do with a note, I pray Mr. Bard didn't read what it said.

🕐🕑🕒🕓🕔

At the end of class, Mr. Bard asks me to stay back for a minute. My eyes widen. I try to gulp but my throat is dry. My heartbeats quicken. This must be about the note.

"What's up Mr. Bard?" I exclaim with as much fake enthusiasm as possible.

"Calm down, Damon. You're not in trouble," Mr. Bard assures me as he walks around the counter and hops up to take a seat in front of me. "How are you doing?"

"Um, fine." I'm not quite sure how to respond because I just watched a middle-aged man hop onto a lab counter as if he were a teenager himself. It was strange.

Mr. Bard clasps his hands, locking his fingers on his lap. "I can't imagine what it is like to have no memories of my childhood so I can't really relate. I can only speak from a position of empathy."

With a confused look, I gaze around the room to make sure I'm not being pranked or something.

"Damon, I'm sorry that you don't know who you are or what happened to you."

"Thank you, Mr. Bard." Although he may be challenging teacher, it's nice when someone else cares enough to reach out to me. "It's hard when I feel like there is no one who can help me. The police did everything they could. The hospital tried their best. Even my psychologist, hasn't been able to pull anything new." I run my finger along the lines of my palm and keep my eyes down. "It's kind of embarrassing."

Mr. Bard jumps down off the counter and walks right up to my desk. His olive gaze presses like it's staring into my soul. "Damon, there is nothing to be embarrassed about. You know as well as I do that this is a scientific problem you are facing. Physiologically speaking, your brain has created a veil, separating you from your past. Perhaps it's even protecting you. I want to encourage you not to give up. You will figure it out. You are too smart to give up now."

"Well, thanks Mr. Bard." I stand up and push my chair in. We face each other. Awkward silence fills the air. Mr. Bard scratches at his solid white goatee and I adjust my backpack straps. "Could you write me a note to English?"

"Oh of course Damon! Of course!" Mr. Bard rushes to his desk and gets out his yellow pass pad and begins scribbling. His short salt and pepper hair shines in the light above his desk. He rips the paper and holds it out for me. "I hope you have a better day, Damon." His crooked smile is full and genuine. I smile back, thank him for the talk, and head down the hall to my next class.

🕐🕑🕒🕓🕔

I amble out to my locker after English class. While putting in my combination, I can't help but feel like I'm being watched. I stop and shoot my head to the right and a group of people disperses in all directions. I return to my task, but the hairs on my neck stand as my ears catch whispers all around me. I turn to the left and spot a group of girls whispering, staring, and even pointing at me.

Do I have something in my teeth? Did I sit in something? Why I am getting so much attention?

Maybe it isn't me they are talking and pointing at. Maybe I'm just paranoid. I exchange books and close my locker. I turn to begin my journey to History Through Film class. All along the halls, people stare. I meet the eyes of a football player and he diverts his gaze to the opposite side of the hall.

Walking faster, it feels like the whispers are getting louder around me. My heart races as anxiety consumes. Imperceptible speech floods my hearing. My pace quickens as I head to the stairs and BAM! I run square into Renner at the door. The collision knocks me to the floor and my books scatter in all directions.

"Whoa, buddy, are you okay?" Renner sounds concerned as he reaches for my notebooks. I look around the hall and those who were lingering hurry to their classes.

The warning bell rings.

"I uh...well...I'm..." I can barely get a word out. The intense, and unwanted, amount of attention I just received threw me for a loop. It reminds me of the police station. The hospital. I'm overwhelmed and don't know what to do.

"Let's go to the nurse's office. You aren't looking too good." Renner grabs my forearm and helps me off the cold tile floor.

I want to say thank you, but nothing is coming out. I look into his eyes with desperation and he responds with a nod. He always knows what I'm trying to say, even when I can't say it.

He gets me to the door of the nurse's office and tells me to wait as he goes inside and speaks with Mrs. Savas, the meanest nurse in the history of high school. While I may not have any memories to compare her to, Renner does and he assures me that she is the worst.

Despite her less than comforting demeanor, Mrs. Savas leans around the side of Renner to look at me and shock fills her face. She rushes over and ushers me to a bed to lay on. I take my glasses off and place them on the table next to me. I hear her say something to Renner about losing color, but by that time my eyes are closed and I fade to sleep.

Coming out of my nap, I can hear Mrs. Savas talking on the phone. I only catch her side of the conversation.

"He must have had a panic attack, Anina…

…Maybe he heard the news and shock overpowered him…"

What news? What is she talking about?

"…Wait, you didn't hear? They found a sixteen-year-old girl in the same abandoned house where Damon was found last year."

I shoot straight up out of the bed, startling Mrs. Savas. She squeals and drops the receiver. I drag my legs off the bed and run out of the office. Mrs. Savas yells down the hall after me, "Damon, come back! Damon!"

Too late.

I'm already out the front doors of the school. I don't know where I'm going, but I know I'm not stopping. It's the middle of the school day, I left my glasses in the nurse's office, and I couldn't care less.

I run through town, passing the blur of businesses and houses. Farmland in one direction, subdivisions in the other. I take lefts and rights. For all I know, I could be running in circles. It doesn't help that my vision is awful.

I end up in front of the Nomad Village Library. Even without my glasses, the two bright, yellow camel statues at the bottom of the stairs are a dead giveaway. I burst through the doors with the sounds of *shhhhh* trailing behind. I reach the back of the building where old cathedral windows stretch from floor to ceiling.

It always blows my mind when I think about the fact that even though glass is solid, I can see through it. The transparent windows cause the light waves to color the room erratically in a blurry kaleidoscope, matching my current mental state.

I plop down in front of a computer and go straight to Google. Lucky for me, I'm near-sighted. I type in "Trevoc" and hit enter. I click the news tab and the first story's headline reads:

SECOND AMNESIC TEEN FOUND IN TREVOC

How is this possible?

My heart was already pounding from the run, but now it dropped into my stomach. I can't breathe. I click the link and read the article.

"Around 4 pm yesterday, a teenage girl was found walking out of an abandoned home in the village of Trevoc. This home has been under heavy surveillance due to random acts of vandalism over the years so the police were quick to pick her up. What is most unusual is that a teenage boy was found in this same home, exactly one year ago.

What makes this seemingly normal breaking-and-entering case so haunting is that this teen, like the first, has no memories of her past. When questioned by police, she could not answer basic questions such as, "What is your name?" and "Where are you from?" She has been transferred to Trevoc Hospital for further questioning, trauma testing, and psychiatric evaluation.

Dr. Maram Habibah released a statement this morning. "What the press needs to understand is that something tragic has happened to this teen and we ask that you respect her privacy in this matter. We do not know yet if her situation is linked to that of last year's, but I can assure you, we will make sure this teen feels safe and secure in our care."

Could it be another case of child abduction? Could this be the work of the same abductors as last year's mystery?

A pattern is emerging in Trevoc and it would be ignorant for the public to believe otherwise."

I blink a few times to assure myself that I'm not having another delusional flash of some sort.

My breathing is shallow and I feel lightheaded. I'm frozen in my seat, unsure of what to do next. As if on autopilot, my feet propel me to the front desk. I ask the librarian if I can use her phone and I dial the one phone number I can think of.

"Could you come pick me up? I'm at the library."

🕐🕑🕐🕔🕕

W e ride in silence for a while. I stare at the floor as the village blurs by in the windows. She didn't ask me anything when I got in the van. I didn't feel like volunteering any information right away.

"Did you know?" I speak, but just above a mumble.

Miss Elle turned her face to me and sniffled. "Yes."

"When did you find out?" My voice raises a tick.

"This morning. You had already left the house. I was in the kitchen when I heard the reporter on the morning news. I ran into the living room, wet hands and all. That's when I found out."

"Why didn't you call the school?" More agitated, my voice is starting to peak.

"Oh Damon. I didn't want to ruin your day. I figured ignorance is bliss until you get home. Then I could sit you down and tell you properly."

My voice jumps with pain. "Would you like to know how I heard?"

"Damon—"

"From the nurse! It wasn't even to my face! I overheard her telling the school secretary about it over the phone!"

Miss Elle yanks the 18-passenger tank to the shoulder of the road, throws it in park, and whips her entire body to face me. My breath catches and my attitude shifts from anger to fear in less than a millisecond.

"You listen to me right now young man. I understand that you are in shock right now, but that is no excuse for disrespect." She turns back toward the steering wheel and uses her sleeve to wipe her nose.

I close my eyes tight for a moment and then loosen. I slide a hand across Miss Elle's shoulder. She jumps, seeming surprised at the gesture. "You're right." She turns to look at me, tears about to spill from her bottom lids. "I'm sorry Miss Elle. I know you were doing what you thought was right."

"You're damn right I was." Miss Elle speaks with a special combination of rigidity and tenderness. She shifts the van back in drive, pulls out of the shoulder, and we head home.

🕐🕑🕒🕓🕔

I wait on the porch for Renner to come home from school. There's something about rocking that is comforting. I'm not sure if it's the motion, the creaking of the chair against the old wooden deck, or both. Whatever it is, I lean my head against the back of the chair, close my eyes, and take advantage of the rare tranquility. The warm breeze is refreshing as it flows through the railing.

I'm in a small room. The blinds are closed, but the moon slips through the slits. My hands are cuffed together around a loop attached to the top of the table. My ankles are heavy from the shackles that bind them. The long mirror on the wall reflects the orange glow of the solitary light hanging over the table.

An officer walks in and sits in the chair across the table from my own. His bare head intensifies the glow of the overhead lamp. His skin is leathery and haggard. He has sunglasses on, despite it being the middle of the night.

I try to lighten the mood. "Is it too bright in here for you, officer?"

"What were you doing in that abandoned house?"

Guess humor isn't his strong suit. Since he doesn't introduce himself to me, I squint in the dark to read his nameplate. "Officer Dennis, I already told you, I don't know. I opened my eyes, looked around, realized I didn't know where I was and started walking. I think I ran into a vase and knocked a picture off the wall. Then you busted down the door and tackled me."

He crosses his arms and leans back in the chair. I can tell his breathing is still labored from the encounter. Officer Dennis is no small man. "How can someone just open their eyes and not remember how they got there?"

"I feel like Stephen King would know the answer to that question—"

He slams a fist down onto the table, causing me to jolt. "Now you listen here, boy. No more games! Who are you and why were you in that house?" His voice booms and echoes around the walls of the small room.

Tossing humor aside, I look at him in desperation. "Officer, if I knew who I was, I would tell you. I have no idea! I don't know my name. I don't know who or where my family is. I don't know how or why I ended up in that house tonight."

He stands up so fast the chair shoots out and falls sideways across the floor. He walks around the table and gets in my face. His hot breath steams up my glasses. "DAMON!"

Like a shot, I sit up in the rocking chair and Renner is staring down at me. He sits on the railing of the porch with a concerned look on his face. The scare hastened my breathing. I lean my elbows on my thighs and place a hand on my forehead.

"Dude, are you okay?" He stretches a hand down toward me, my glasses in palm.

I shove them on and sigh. "Just another nightmare. This time I was at the police station."

"Brutal." He leans back on the railing to grab an apple from the tree and crunches into it. I notice the flesh of the fruit has a green tint. "I heard you went nuts in the nurses' office and ran." His mouth drools full with apple bits.

"That about sums it up."

After a few chews, he makes a sour face, spits the apple guts into the bushes next to him, and chucks the rest into the yard. I stifle a laugh. I thought about warning him that the apple wasn't ripe, but I'm glad I didn't.

"I knew people were whispering in the halls, but I figured you just did something to embarrass yourself. After I left you in the nurses' office, I was in Trig when Bob from archery told me the news about the girl. I asked if I could be excused to the bathroom and ran downstairs to find you. Mrs. Savas caught me on the way and told me you jumped out of bed and ran out of the school." He pauses for a while. "Damon, if I had known sooner, you know I would've told you. Sorry you had to hear it from that hag."

I lean back in the chair and rock, giving him a slight smile. "I know. I appreciate that."

We stare as one comrade to another. Then the stare shifts to awkwardness and Renner searches around us for a response. "Welp, I'll leave you with your thoughts." He jumps down off the railing, gives me a slap on the shoulder, and enters the house.

I think I would be lost without Renner.

Despite my whole ordeal, my mind wanders to how the girl they found is doing. If she's experiencing anything like I did last year, she's in hell right now. No memories. Strangers questioning you. Prodding. Testing. Scanning. The press wants information causing chaos everywhere you go. It's awful.

I'm also curious to see if there's a link between her and I and our happenstance. The other part of me is terrified to find out the truth. What if it's like what Dr. Habibah said? What if what happened to me was so traumatic that my brain is blocking it out to protect me?

What if my life would be worse for knowing?

Two little hands covering my eyes interrupt my thoughts.

"Guess who?"

I chuckle. "I'm going to guess that it's someone who likes getting chased by the tickle monster."

Viv giggles behind me. "No way!"

She pulls her hands away and runs to the front of the chair, laughing. "No silly! It's me, Viv!"

"I knew it! You better run, the tickle monster is going to get you." I extend my hands to grab her, but she bolts inside. I hesitate for a second and then dash through the door before Viv can find a good hiding place.

IV

"She hasn't returned my calls from last night or this morning." I watch Renner shove another spoonful of cereal in his mouth.

"Didn't the article say she was at Trevoc Hospital working with the girl? Maybe we could go over there after school so you can track her down in person?"

I stare down at my half-eaten muffin and cringe a little. "The thought of going back to school after my 'episode' yesterday makes me want to return this muffin to its original, but more acidic, state."

Viv chimes in, her mouth full of oatmeal, "Gross."

Renner reaches across with a fist and Viv pounds it. He swallows his last bite. "If it's that big of a deal, convince Miss Elle to take you the hospital during school today."

"I can't ask her to do that. She can't leave the babies. Yesterday, the neighbor had to come watch them so she could pick me up from the library. I think it's going to be a long time before I ask Miss Elle for any more favors."

Miss Elle appears in the doorway between the dining room and the kitchen, drying off a dish. "Renner, didn't you tell me you weren't feeling well this morning?"

Renner puts down his cereal bowl after chugging the milk. "Huh?"

"Don't you lie to me, mister. I already called the school and told them you two were ill, so you and Damon better go straight back to bed because you both will return to school tomorrow! And Viv go brush your teeth so you can catch the bus." Viv gives a tiny salute and leaves the table. Miss Elle picks up the oatmeal bowl and disappears into the kitchen. Renner shoots a confused gaze at me and I shrug. We stand to collect our dishes and hear yelling. "And don't you think for a second that I'll leave my van keys out on the coffee table. No joy rides for you two."

We enter the kitchen to put our dishes in the dishwasher and Miss Elle has already vanished. I turn to Renner and he's smiling. A large, goofy smile. It's kinda scary. He laughs in response to my fear-stricken face. "You haven't known Miss Elle for as long as I have." He leads me to the couch room. The van keys sit in the middle of the coffee table holding down a twenty-dollar bill. He scoops it all up. "Let's go."

🕐🕑🕒🕓🕔

"I can't believe she let us skip school like that." I stare out the window toward the Trevoc Hospital entrance.

Renner rests his left arm out the window, letting the autumn breeze flow through his jacket sleeve. "Miss Elle has dealt with a lot of things through the years. Abuse, trauma, neglect, abandonment. You though, Damon, you are whole different bird."

"Yeah, I'm quite an anomaly." I'm not sure how I feel about that.

Renner reaches across and slaps me in the ribs. "Come on man. Quit taking things so personally."

I rub my ribs to try to squeeze some guilt out of Renner, but it doesn't work. "In all seriousness, Miss Elle has been running the children's home for years and suddenly she's stuck with a teenage boy who has no memories, at least not of the past."

"I guess that would be weird." Renner parks the van, turns off the engine, and plays with the zipper on his jacket. "Have you ever thought about the fact that you can walk, talk, read, and do complex scientific equations but have no idea when your birthday is or if you've ever had chicken pox?"

"All the time."

Renner gives an audible, impatient sigh. "Well, are you just going to sit here or are you going in?"

"Now or never I guess."

"I'll be here, taking a nap. I'm not your getaway driver so behave in there." Renner laughs as he puts back the driver's seat and closes his eyes.

All hospitals are similar. Clean lines. Clear signs. The glass double doors open automatically. The strong scent of bleach and formaldehyde at every step. I walk up to the check-in counter and a woman with dark complexion holds up her finger as she finishes up a call. She stares through her hot pink reading glasses to write on the pad in front of her. Hanging up the phone, she pulls her glasses down to hang around her neck. "How can I help you dear?"

"I'm here to see Dr. Habibah."

She looks down the hallway to her right and back to me. "How did you know she was here today? Do you have an appointment?" She clicks through her computer.

"No, I'm a patient and I've tried to get ahold of her a few times but—"

"I'm sorry son, I'm going to stop you there. Dr. Habibah is not seeing any of her usual patients until further notice."

I close my eyes tight and sigh. "Please ma'am. If you could just tell her who I am, I'm sure she'll—"

"No." She stands up, much broader than she looked sitting down, and crosses her arms. "Dr. Habibah will contact you when she is available." Putting her hot pink reading glasses back on her nose, she flops into her chair and continues writing her notes.

I meander toward the exit. My ear catches the sound of mumbling over a radio. The woman behind the desk responds, but not loud enough for me to decipher what is being said. I sneak a peek over my shoulder. She's gone.

This is my chance.

I rush back to the desk. I take a left turn down the hall the nurse was so quick to look down when blocking me from Dr. Habibah. When I get to the hall, there are dozens of doors marked with numbers. She could be in any of these rooms. I walk normally so the orderlies won't think anything suspicious. I take unnoticeable pauses in front of each door so maybe I'll overhear her talking. Dr. Habibah's accent is hard to miss, but these doors are thick.

I continue down the corridor, trying not to draw attention to myself, when door 1111 opens and Dr. Habibah walks out, almost running into me. She shuts the door behind her, eyes wide. "What are you doing here, Damon?"

"I've been trying to call you." It's been more like blowing up her phone.

"You shouldn't be here."

"I know. I heard the news." Why doesn't she want to help me?

She keeps her hands behind her back on the door handle, like she could escape at any moment. "Damon. You, of all people, should know what this girl is going through. She needs my undivided attention right now."

"I've been having more nightmares and seeing things that aren't there." The words slip out in a more desperate tone than I was planning.

"Damon." Her hands release from the door handle. "I know this is probably a shocking time for you considering everything. I'll make a deal with you. If you continue to do your visualization and breathing exercises like I've taught you and stay in Nomad, I promise I will meet with you at the beginning of next week."

She holds out a hand. I stare at it feeling like a second-rate patient, but if this is all I get, I guess I better take it. "Deal." We shake. She gives me a small smile and says goodbye. When she opens the door, I glance in the room and there she is. Sitting at the end of the bed, the girl's body swims in a baggy hospital gown, feet dangling with ankle high socks. Her hair is long and fiery. Her right hand pulls some hair behind her ear and I catch the shimmer of a ring. Her dark eyes meet mine a moment before the door shuts.

Chills run down my spine.

The split-second encounter causes me to lose balance and I fall backwards against the far wall. My vision flickers like a strobe. I'm brought to my knees. I squeeze my eyes shut and my head pounds. I open my eyes, but something's wrong. Everything goes black. I try not to panic at my sudden blindness when I notice my other senses heightening. The air is cold and smells sterile. My hands reach for my chest and feel the scratchiness of a polyester gown. My hearing kicks on like an unmuted TV and a flood of sound assaults me. A beeping heart monitor, clanging metal, many voices speaking in panicked tones. A woman screams amid the chaos and it makes my breath catch. In an instant, all sounds mute. After a few seconds, a faint, low cry breaks the silence and grows louder and more repetitive. I don't know why, but I sigh in relief. I feel something shove me from behind and as I turn, my sight snaps back on. Renner looks lost.

"Dude, I'm hungry. Ugh, why are you all sweaty? Did you get to see Dr. Habibah?"

I blink and fight to catch my breath. I take my glasses off and rub my eyes. I get up from the floor of the hallway and turn to Renner. "I saw her briefly. I also caught a glimpse of the girl. Then I couldn't see anything at all…"

"Okay. Tell me about it on the way to Rally's. I want some fries."

🕐🕑🕒🕓🕔

Renner keeps glancing over at me. He's probably irritated that I haven't said anything to him since he found me in the hall of the hospital. Or he could be concerned. I guess I'm not very good at reading people. Especially when they are driving.

"You've had long enough to think, Damon. What happened in there?"

"Remember how I had that weird flash in the bathroom at the home?"

"The one where you saw an older dude in the mirror? Yeah."

"Well I had something similar happen in the hospital. This time I couldn't see anything, but I could tell I was in a hospital room with a screaming woman."

Renner turns off the radio and returns his hand to the steering wheel. "I know I joked about you becoming a psychopath, but have you thought about what this could mean?"

"I was really hoping Dr. Habibah could tell me what it all meant. The visions *feel* real."

"What do you mean?"

"Like I've experienced them. As if, I've seen and heard those people before."

"Wait. Are you getting memories back?"

I take my glasses off and rest them on my leg. I push my

fingers into my eyes hard until my vision is blurry and multicol-ored. I slide my fingers down my face. "I don't know. Maybe. All I know is when that girl looked at me, the flash happened. That can't be coincidental, can it?"

"It sounds like she sparked a memory of some sort."

I turn my gaze to Renner. "I have this feeling in the pit of my stomach. It's twisty and anxious. My visions are familiar to me. Maybe the guy I saw and the things I heard relate to my abduction."

"Holy crap on a cracker." Renner laughs nervously. "This is crazy. What are you going to do?"

"I don't know. Dr. Habibah said she would meet with me at the beginning of next week so maybe I'll just wait until then to decide."

This is too much to process. I close my eyes and lean my seat back, willing us to get home quicker so I can curl up in bed to sleep this off.

🕐🕑🕐🕓🕔

I follow a man to the back of the precinct. My steps labor as the shackles around my ankles restrict my stride. He closes and locks the door to a room where a lonely computer resides. The room is cold and bare. The officer leads me to the desk, clicks a few things on the screen. "Since we already ran your description through our missing person's database and came up empty, I'm going to take an electronic scan of your fingerprints. We'll run them through our civil and criminal databases and maybe this will help us identify who you are."

Below the computer screen is a large gray box with a small portion sticking out from the bottom right corner. He flips the cover and reveals a small, backlit screen. He takes a disinfecting wipe from the tub next to the screen and cleans my right hand. He grasps my right thumb and instructs me not to help him move it during the scan, but that he would *do it for me. The officer carefully rolls my thumb across the glass from right to left. He looks at the screen and the word REJECT pops up in red next to what looks like a dark smudge. The officer sighs and tries again, this time cleaning the glass as well as my thumb. He rolls my thumb again and the same results display. Angry, he clicks hard to reset. After a few more attempts trying a different finger, a different hand, using more pressure, adding lotion, and slowing down the rolls, the officer shuts off the machine, mumbling something about not getting paid enough.*

Leading me out of the back room, the officer brings me to a small brown table. "I guess we're doing this the old-fashioned way." My fingers turn through the ink and onto the cards, but when I look down, my prints are solid. No ridges. No lines.

I look at my fingers and can see where the skin rises and falls. The officer inspects my fingers carefully. The deputy stands up and stares me in the eyes. "Are you messing with me kid?"

I swallow hard. "What? How could I be messing with you? You are taking the prints. I haven't done anything, just like you instructed."

The young, obviously irritated, deputy yells out the door for his superior. Another man enters the room and takes me through the same routine. He even recalibrated the electronic scanner for good measure. Same results. The seasoned officer glances up at me. Instead of rage, he shows pity. He puts a hand on my shoulder. "I'm sorry young man. We will not be able to identify you through this process. Let's go to the holding room so I can call a friend of mine at the hospital to assist us."

After exiting the fingerprinting area, he cuffs me back to the table where Officer Dennis harassed me earlier. I can hear talking outside the door. The young deputy said something that I couldn't make out, but the seasoned officer's words were loud and clear. "Unfortunately, if this kid doesn't get his memories back, he may never know who he is."

My eyes open, releasing me from a familiar nightmare. I fell asleep on the couch waiting for dinner. The house is quiet so everyone must be in bed already. The faint sound of clicking grabs my attention. Miss Elle knits in her chair as the colors from the muted television dance around her. Doc is delivering his iconic line in *Back to the Future Part II*, "The time-traveling is just too dangerous. Better that I devote myself to study the other great mystery of the universe: women!" I've watched this trilogy so often in this past year that I don't need the sound. I've memorized most of the lines.

"Are you all right, young man?"

"Yes, Miss Elle." I sit up on the couch, realizing a blanket was laid on me.

She looks at me over her glasses. "Don't lie."

"I've been having more nightmares and what can only be described as flashes. What if I never remember who I am, Miss Elle?" I sigh.

"What if you don't? What then?"

"I guess I just go on with life as it is now?"

"Is that what you want, Damon?" She takes off her glasses and places them and her knitting on the side table.

"I don't know. When I heard the officer say that I might never know who I am, you know what I wanted to do?"

"No. What?"

"I wanted to run away. Isn't that childish?" I trace the lines on in my right hand with my thumb and stare into floor.

Miss Elle, stands, walks over to the couch, and sits next to me. "No. Everyone has instincts, Damon, fight or flight instincts. It makes sense that you wanted to run away in that moment."

"To be honest, when I arrived at the home I was ready to run away that night too."

"Why didn't you?"

"It didn't make sense anymore. If I ran, where would I go? I don't know who I am or where my family is. Where would I stay? What would I do? You were a big reason why I stayed, Miss Elle."

Although the darkness is broken by the flashes of the muted

television, I can tell she is blushing. "Well you certainly know how to flatter an old lady."

"It's true! You were so warm and accepting. Then Renner treated me like a brother the moment I got here. Like I said, it didn't make sense to run."

"And now?"

I look Miss Elle deep into her eyes. "Now I want to fight. Renner and I talked and I think my memory flashes are about my captors."

Miss Elle's eyes widen. "You do?"

"I want to know what happened. If I can figure out who my kidnappers were, maybe I will get my memories back. Maybe I will finally find out who I am and what happened to me."

I see her head drop out of the corner of my eye. "What if it's awful, Damon? What if what they did to you was horrific?"

"I think that's a chance I'm willing to take now."

"How are you going to find them? The police did all they could and came up empty."

"The girl. When she looked at me, I felt something familiar. I think there is something to that. We are connected somehow. Dr. Habibah said she might meet with me Monday, but I'm going to call her tomorrow to ask if I can speak to the girl."

"Damon, remember what it was like after you were found? Everything you went through?"

I grab Miss Elle's soft, wrinkly hand and nod. "If I can convince her that working together could restore our memories, she might be willing to help."

Miss Elle squeezes my hand. "All right, Damon Doe. Just be careful. Everyone reacts differently to the same news."

"I will. Goodnight, Miss Elle."

"Goodnight dear."

V

Friday, September 8, 2017

I plug my ear to try to hear her voice over the phone. Some of the littles are playing a loud game of tag in the couch room where I'm talking to Dr. Habibah.

"No."

"You haven't even heard why I want to meet with her."

"I don't need to, Damon. It would be too overwhelming. She's been through so much in just a few days."

The kids scream louder. I stuff myself into the corner of the room between the wall and the desk to try to find relief from the noise. The curly phone cord is stretched to its max from the wall mount above me. "Let's think about this reasonably. You are faced with a patient that has gone through a trauma causing dissociative amnesia. You have a patient you've been working with for a year with the same exact issue, who was found in the same exact place. Don't you think it would make logical sense to have us meet to work out what's happened together?"

I can't tell if Dr. Habibah is silent or if the room got louder. I poke my head out and yell. "Viv is in the dining room everyone!"

Like a herd of wild animals, they stampede out of the couch room. Viv pokes her head out from under the desk, winks at me, and then sneaks through the kitchen door. The room finally quiets.

"I'll think about it, Damon. I have an appointment with her now. I'll contact you if anything changes."

The call ends before I can say goodbye. There's nothing more I can do but wait.

♻♻♻♻♻

Saturday, September 9, 2017

I know I've been in this room many times, but I've never really looked around. Dr. Habibah's desk is a dark wood, delicate with ornate swirls and hardware. The bookcase on the right side of the room is filled with books on psychology and counseling. The left wall has a very large aquarium filled with various tropical fish like blue tangs and clown fish. A large window behind her desk allows for a flood of natural light and an impressive view of a sunflower field in full bloom. I take a deep breath. The room smells of lavender, though I can't figure out where the scent is coming from. I'm just glad it doesn't smell like fish or a hospital.

As I trace the lines in my palms, I realize I'm just spreading sweat through the cracks. I rub my hands on my jeans and rest them on the table. Anxiety has been creeping up on me all week. Now it stands heavy on my chest, a reminder that what I'm doing is risky. The outcome of this meeting is unknown and that is what stabs at me most.

Dr. Habibah opens the door behind me and I turn in my chair. The girl's russet hair floats around her as she edges toward the seat next to me. I stand up out of polite gesture and a bit of nervous awkwardness. Black Chuck Taylors, black leggings, and a purple flannel shirt covers her body, instead of the itchy hospital gown I saw her in two days before. She rubs the pearl button on her cuff and I realize I've been sizing her up. I shake my head and stammer, "I'm—I'm sorry for staring. I'm Damon."

Her dark eyes look at me but I can't read her. "Yeah. Dr. Habibah told me."

Dr. Habibah coughs from the doorway, drawing our attention to her. She speaks solely to the girl. "I'll be in the lobby when you are ready to go back to Trevoc, okay?"

The girl nods her head and Dr. Habibah leaves with a simple close of the door. I extend a hand to the seat next to me and we sit, slightly turned toward one another.

Tucking a strand of hair behind her ear, her ring catches my eye again. The stone glows purple in a recognizable way. She puts her hands in her lap before I can take in any more of its details. She spins the ring clockwise on her finger and sighs with a nervous catch. "I've decided to go by Nori."

My eyebrows jump. "That's a beautiful name."

Why did I say that out loud?

"That's what I thought too. I know it is a type of Japanese seaweed, but they put me on the spot."

"I know what that's like." I smile awkwardly. She doesn't seem phased by my outburst so that's promising. My smile fades as I remember the day I chose my name. "I'm surprised Dr. Habibah agreed to this meeting. She shot me down yesterday when I suggested it on the phone."

Nori tucks more hair behind her ear, staring down at the front of Dr. Habibah's desk. "It took a lot of convincing for her to bring me here."

She wanted to come?

I wipe my forehead with my sleeve, knowing full well I could've picked something better to wear than my worn-out NASA t-shirt.

"When I saw you in the hospital, Nori, I felt something."

"What?" Her eyes dart up to mine with a flash of fear beneath.

"No. Okay. What I mean is when I looked at you it felt familiar. Like I already knew you."

"Damon, I don't think—"

"After that split second of seeing you, I had some kind of memory flash—"

"Damon—"

"I think our stories are connected."

"I'm not ready!" Her eyes dart to the left toward the windows. Every time I watch crime shows, they say that is a tell-tale sign of lying. "I really am sorry, but I don't know you. I don't even know myself."

"That's just it!" My voice echoes louder in this office than I remember. I lower my voice. "What are the odds that two teens, around the same age, are found in the same abandoned building with no memories of their past?"

She seems to sink into her chair more. "I told you I'm sorry. This is going too fast for me."

"Did you know we were found on the same day one year apart? I was found on September 5th, 2016 and you were found on September 5th, 2017. It all lines up." I'm out of breath, working hard to get all my thoughts out without scaring her more.

"What time?"

"What do you mean?"

"What time did they find you?"

I scratch my head. "When they put me in the police car, the clock said 11:15pm. I was only in the house for a few minutes before being taken into custody."

Nori sighs and sits back up in her seat. "I was found at 4pm so that means the times don't match."

I shake my head, growing impatient. "That's what you are going to focus on? Time makes everything else coincidental?"

Her jaw stiffens. "Dr. Habibah tried to warn me not to have this meeting, but I didn't listen."

This is not going at all how I hoped. "Don't you want to know who you are or what happened to you, Nori?"

"Damon, I woke up four days ago in a dank and dusty house. I don't even know my own name. The police interrogated me. The doctors prodded and ran tests on me. I'm still trying to process everything. It was a mistake coming here." She wipes a tear from her eye with a flannel sleeve and stands up.

"Nori, please wait." I stand so fast, my chair crashes to the floor.

"Goodbye, Damon." She turns around; her flaming hair floats around her as she moves toward the door.

I grab my chair, set it back up, and try to catch up to her. I'm not trying to scare her, but I want her to understand. She gets to the lobby and Dr. Habibah shuts the book she was reading. I yell out to her. "I've spent a year of my life in the dark."

She turns her head so one eye peers over her shoulder.

"Do you want to wait another year before you remember who you are? I'm sorry if it seems like I'm pushing you into this, but I know there's a connection between us and I think you know it too."

Nori turns toward me so I can see her entire face. She purses her lips together and the down-turned corners of her mouth signal remorse. She lifts a hand away from her crossed arms to wave as she turns back to Dr. Habibah. They walk together through the lobby and exit the glass sliding doors. She doesn't look back.

🕐🕑🕒🕓🕔

"**B**ummer." Renner's arrow strikes the target in perfect time with his retort. It's weird to see him without his khaki jacket on. He's practicing in a new team archery shirt for competitions. The shirt is a deep purple with gold stripes down the sleeves, from neck to wrist. The front has the words Nomad High Archery Team wrapped around an illustration of a target, the back says EMIT in bright gold lettering.

I bury my head in my hands. "I really thought she'd want to know. I thought she would want to work together to figure out what happened to us. Instead, I think I scared her off."

"Well you probably could've dressed a little nicer, my astronaut brother."

"Renner! I'm serious!"

"Damon! You're always serious!" He sighs loud, for my benefit I guess.

"This is my life we're talking about. This is so selfish of her."

"Wait what?" Renner rolls his eyes. "The girl wakes up and a few days later meets a guy who went through the same thing she did. I don't blame her for wanting to run far away from this one. It's not selfishness, it's self-preservation." Renner walks down to the target and yanks out the arrow. "Put yourself in her shoes except be girly about it. She, like you, is the possible victim of abduction. Wouldn't it be easier just to forget and move on than open what could be an insane can of worms?"

I shake my head. "You don't understand."

He stops mid stride, clenches the arrow in his hand, and squeezes his eyes shut. "Oh, I don't?"

I sense his agitation, but I decide to poke the bear anyway. "You wouldn't have the first idea about what I've been going through this year."

The bear, as expected, advances on me and I stand still, ready for the attack. "You know what? I've been pretty quiet this past week because I'm your friend and you've had a lot on your plate, but your whining has put me over the edge." Renner's chest presses into mine as his dark eyes glare downward into mine. "You are not the only person on Earth with problems. My parents *abandoned* me. The only memories I have from childhood are of my grandmother reading me poems and then *dying*. I remember putting a rose on her grave at five-years-old, Damon. I came to the children's home and have never been considered for fostering or adoption. At this point, I've aged out of ever having a family. Don't tell me I don't understand. I have no memories of my childhood because I was not granted the luxury of having one. I don't know what happened to my parents and probably never will." He pushes his body through me, causing me to fall into the grass. He doesn't look back either.

VI

Monday, September 11, 2017

The florescent lights exacerbate my headache. Seething anger radiates from my best friend across the aisle, unaware if I can even still call him that anymore. It's been two days since we've spoken to each other. Childish. Mr. Bard drones on like the teacher from the Charlie Brown cartoons, *wah wah wah*. I shut my eyes for a moment and sigh. I open them and spot Nori in the doorway of the classroom. I shake my head and blink a few times to make sure it's not just in my head. It's real. Our school guidance counselor leads her into the room.

"Excuse the interruption, Mr. Bard. You will have a new student in your class for a few weeks until we can get a more suitable schedule put together. This is Nori."

The room pauses. Everyone sits quiet, frozen, as if holding their breath at the same time. I look over at Renner. I know he's still mad at me, but this is so shocking, I need a reaction from him. His eyes stare wide into the middle of his paper. Rigid and unblinking, Renner resembles a store mannequin. I reach across the aisle and smack his arm. He shakes his head as if breaking from a trance and I mouth *that's her*. Still wide-eyed he nods, turning his gaze back to our new classmate.

Mr. Bard motions to the one open seat in the room, right behind me. Nori holds her books close to her chest as she makes her way to her new seat. The atmosphere around me changes. I no longer feel the heat from Renner's direction. The air is electrified. I catch her sweet smell as she floats by me and I turn my concentration toward not blushing

It isn't working.

Fortunately for me, when I'm embarrassed or flustered, only my ears turn red. Normally Renner would notice, but he's staring at the board.

The guidance counselor leaves, our science teacher returns to his discussion of genomics, and I'm frozen in my seat. Her proximity makes the hairs on my neck stand on end. I feel something glide along my back between my shoulder blades. Trying not to make too much of a scene, I shift my eyes to the left and turn my head until I see a small pink paper resting against my shoulder. I reach up with my right hand and casually scratch my shoulder, retrieving the note from her waiting fingers. I bring my hands beneath the lab table to open the note. One solitary word is written in dainty script. If someone saw this note they wouldn't think anything of it, but I think the world of it. All it says is, "Okay."

🕐🕑🕒🕓🕔

The air is crisp on my walk back to the home. The tops of the trees are showing signs of chlorophyll breakdown as the leaves begin their seasonal changes. I try to concentrate on the complexity of changing daylight and temperature and its effect on fall foliage, but that little pink note feels like it's burning a hole in my sweatshirt pocket. I reach in to warm up my hands, or so I convince myself. Running my fingers along the edge of the note, the anticipation builds in my fingertips and spreads to my already pounding heart. Ever since I got this note, my heart hasn't stopped racing. Nori left class in such a hurry, we didn't get to talk. Throughout the school day, I caught glimpses of her crimson hair wafting around corners, but couldn't catch up to her.

I count my steps on the sidewalk when I bump into the backpack of a person walking in front of me. Shuffling around, I apologize and look up to meet Renner's dark eyes. He stops for a second, but then keeps walking. I raise my voice so he can hear me through the rustling trees. "I mean it."

Renner stops and turns to face me. There's about five feet of distance between us, but it feels so much farther considering our last conversation. "You mean what exactly?"

"I'm sorry for running into you and for being so selfish."

He zips his jacket up to his chin and crosses his arms. With the sun setting around him, his silhouette rises above me. "Fine." His voice bellows.

I squint my eyes. "And that means?"

He walks over to me, a shadow growing larger and larger, and puts a hand on my shoulder. "It means you need to tell me what's in that note or I'm going to hurt you."

I sigh and smile in relief. He gives me a half smile. I know he's trying to move past our fight and I'm thankful for that. It doesn't feel like I'm forgiven yet, but I deserve that. I'm just happy he's talking to me.

🕐🕑🕒🕓🕔

We reach the gate to the home and I see Nori rocking on the front porch with a dirt smeared Viv sitting in her lap. I look at Renner and he shrugs. Our expressions match as we try to figure out why she's here. We reach the front steps when Dr. Habibah steps out the front door. Viv jumps off Nori's lap and runs into my arms. I squeeze her tight. I always look forward to after school Viv squeezes. She then jumps to Renner and climbs him like a spider monkey.

"This must be Renner Emit. I've heard a lot about you." She reaches out to shake his hand. She's a corgi compared to Renner's mastiff size. "It seems Pilut was the only children's home in a 100-mile radius of Trevoc with an empty bed—"

"Oh yeah!" Renner interrupts. "Last week little Asa was adopted into a nice family. I'm going to miss her. She used to moon people all the time." Viv chuckles loud from atop Renner's shoulders.

I may or may not have taught her that, but I'm not admitting to anything.

"Well because of that, Nori will be staying here until more permanent accommodations are found." She turns to Nori. "Miss Elle assured me that if she could handle one amnesic kid, she can certainly handle two," Dr. Habibah giggles. I've never heard her giggle before. It's weird. "Anyway, I'm going to head back to Trevoc. The two of you have my number if you need anything." Dr. Habibah walks out to her white, yet dirt-covered, BMW and drives away.

Viv, still balancing on Renner's shoulders, climbs down. She runs back over to Nori and bounces into her lap, a little too hard. For a six-year-old, Viv has a boney tush. Nori masks the sudden impact with a bright, toothy smile. "Damon, have you met Nori yet?"

"Yes, Viv, I've met Nori."

"Good. She's really sweet *and* pretty. Don't you think, Damon?"

My eyes are now the size of saucers. Renner pats me on the shoulder, laughs, and heads inside. My throat is dry as I try to force air and words out. "Um, yeah Viv. Why don't you go inside and wash up for dinner?"

"Is that so you can talk to Nori alone?"

"No, it's because you are covered in who-knows-what and you know how Miss Elle gets when you are filthy at dinnertime."

Viv turns in Nori's lap and locks her in a close gaze. "She gets really cranky if I'm dirty at the table. Gotta go!" The little one slides down and gallops inside, leaving Nori and I alone.

I walk onto the porch and sit down in the chair next to her and rock. I wish talking to girls was as easy as rocking on a porch.

"This is weird, isn't it?"

I stop rocking. "It's only weird if we make it weird."

"I've thought a lot about what you said. I don't want to wait a year before memories start coming back. We have a rare opportunity to find out what happened to us. I pushed for Dr. Habibah to let me stay here in Nomad and go to school with you so we could be closer." I swivel my head in surprise and her face flushes red. "Wait. What I meant was that we'd be closer in proximity."

"Uh huh. Sure. That's what you meant." I raise my eyebrows and stand up to cross my arms.

Wait, am I flirting?

"Damon!" she laughs. "You knew what I meant."

Is she flirting, too?

I tilt my head and shrug my shoulders. "I don't know. It certainly sounded like something else to me."

Miss Elle pops her head out the front door. "You two better get inside or there won't be any chili or cornbread left."

"Thanks, Miss Elle," Nori says as she stands up. "Let's just forget I said anything, okay?"

"Nope. I'm never going to let you live it down." She punches me in the arm and walks into the house. I stand, but my heart starts pounding and my vision flickers. I blink my eyes. I'm becoming more familiar with what happens when a memory flash is coming. I close my eyes tight and when I open them I see a large lecture hall with hundreds of chairs. I walk down the steps to the bottom and sit in the front row. A few minutes later I hear petite steps near me. A body slides into the seat to my right. I don't turn my head right away, but out of the corner of my eye, I can see it.

Fiery red hair.

The lights flash again and I feel Viv's body hanging around my waist and her little voice yelling. "Come eat, Damon! It's yummy!" Reality is restored and I walk into the house a little more confused but happy with the possibilities ahead.

🕐🕑🕒🕓🕔

Tuesday, September 12, 2017

My sandwich is pulverized in my mouth because frankly, I have no idea what to say. Nori is staring at me from across the lunch table, as silent as I am. We've geared up to tackle our problems together, but now that we're in the game, it's difficult to know what to do or say next. The crunch of her carrots seems deafening in our bubble of silence. The cafeteria is bustling with noises of laughter, whiffs of pizza and chocolate milk, and students walking around and settling in with their factions. I'm startled out of our awkward dining by the flop of Renner in the chair next to me.

"So, what are we going to do now?" Renner takes a large bite of his square pizza. He lets the cheese string out until it rips and sticks to his chin.

"Well, I was thinking we could go to Trevoc, where we were found."

Nori perks up. "Yes! That's a great idea. We could search for answers there!"

"What does that mean though? *Search for answers?* Do you even know what your questions are?" Renner makes a good point, but I don't want to inflate his ego too much.

"I started writing questions down last night since I couldn't sleep," Nori interrupts before I can speak.

"Oh?"

"Yeah, those bunk beds are too squeaky and Miss Elle's snoring. Yikes."

Renner and I smile at each other and say simultaneously, "You get used it."

She slides her notebook across the table and Renner reads aloud.

"Were the circumstances of our discovery similar? Were there any suspicious marks found on our bodies? Was any other DNA found?"

"Great start, Nori!" I smile at her and feel my ears burn. I reach up and itch the one closest to Renner so he doesn't suspect anything.

"Thanks!" She stuffs another carrot into her mouth without hesitation.

Renner furrows his brow, narrowing his eyes as he watches my fervent scratching. Looking back down at the list, he pulls out a pen and writes the word, *Who?*

"Okay, while these questions may be a good start, you two really need to figure out who it is you are going to ask. Trevoc is 90 miles away. You don't want to get there and end up wasting time because you didn't have a plan. Decide who the most important people to talk to are and then you can work your way around town."

Renner is right. Again. I guess I should give him credit. "You're right."

"I know. I'm the brains of this group." Renner throws back his head and chugs his milk. As he does, dribbles streak down from the corners of his mouth.

I regret my decision.

"Hey genius, you missed your mouth." Nori laughs as she points to his soaking shirt. She laughs so hard she snorts a little, causing me to spit out my chips and join her. Renner uses the dry part of his collar to clean his chin and neck and snickers beneath the cloth.

🕐🕑🕓🕔🕕

Nori and I meet in the library after school so we can better discuss our plans. Renner couldn't come since he's prepping for an archery tournament, but I don't mind. Nori sits next to me, her scent sweet and our privacy cherished.

"Damon, as much as I hate to admit it, Renner was right. We need to figure out who to talk to so we aren't just wandering around."

"He can be a dolt sometimes but he's my best friend and does have some wisdom in that head of his."

Nori pulls out her notebook and turns to the questions page and looks at the giant *Who?* Renner wrote earlier. "Let's think back to when we were found. While that may not be long ago for me, it was over a year ago for you."

"Believe me, my brain doesn't let me forget that."

"Good! I mean—no, that's not what I meant." She fiddles with her pen for a minute. I can tell she's trying to figure out how to recover but she pushes through. "I remember what the officer looked like who found me in the house. Do you remember who found you?"

I stare up at the dusty books on the encyclopedia shelves. I didn't realize talking this out might actually be worse than just having nightmares about it. "His last name was Dennis. After tackling me to the ground, he interrogated me for a few hours before giving up and calling a different officer to take my fingerprints."

Nori looks at me wide-eyed and surprised. "I'm sorry you were tackled. I walked out the front door and the officer saw me near the mailbox. He got out and asked me who I was and why I was in front of that house. He was a bit gentler with me, I guess maybe because I'm a girl. I don't think my officer was named Dennis. He could still work at the precinct though."

"You don't remember the name of your officer?"

"No." Nori stares around the bookshelves too. Her pain is more recent than mine. "I was pretty scared because it was like I just woke up, like I was reborn or something. A flash of light blinds me and then I'm in a dark house. I don't know who I am or how I got there. It didn't take me long to decide to leave, but it did take a bit of persuasion on the officer's part to go with him."

"I understand." I hate remembering that night.

"I'm sorry, Damon." Her gaze casts to the floor. She spins the purple gem clockwise on her hand.

"Why?"

"I guess this is harder than we thought."

I take a chance and put my hand on her forearm. "No. We're together now and we're going to figure this out."

She sets her hand on top of mine. It's soft and warm. "Okay."

We linger for what feels like eternity. She looks down and jerks her hand to grab her pen. A lefty. I take my hand away from her forearm to ease the awkwardness, though deep inside I don't want to. She writes down the name Dennis under the *Who?*

"Next?" She taps her pen on the page.

"Since everything is still fresh in your mind, what happened next?"

Nori bites the inside of her cheek. "They tried to take my

fingerprints. It was weird. They used the electronic machine first, but it kept showing an error. Then when they tried to use ink—"

"Everything was smudged!"

"Yes!" Nori yells. The librarian's head shoots up faster than a dog when asked if it wants food and shushes us. We duck our heads from view and revert to whispering. "You too?"

"Yep."

"Did they try to do a DNA test on you too?"

"I don't remember."

"Well, they took a strand of my hair and put it through whatever program they use to get DNA to try to match it to someone in the database. It came back inconclusive though. They tried blood to be extra sure. All I ended up with was a bad bruise from the medical student with a shaky hand."

"Do you remember who he was?"

"No, but I doubt he'd be any help. The chief of medicine yelled at him for doing such a poor job so he left in a hurry."

"What about after the police station?"

"They took me to the Trevoc Hospital." Nori picks at her fingers and returns to chewing her cheek. "They told me they needed to run tests on me to make sure I was okay."

"What do you mean?"

"They didn't tell me they were going to run a rape kit until right before they did it." She stops chewing her cheek and sinks in her chair.

"Oh, Nori. I'm so sorry." I am. I think this was worse for her than it was for me.

"Actually, they had Dr. Habibah come in to tell me. She was assuring me that no one would harm me and that she was there to help me figure out who I am and what happened. That's when I saw you."

"Oh. You remember that?" My throat closes.

"Of course. When you're sitting in an itchy hospital gown

getting ready for an awkward procedure, you remember seeing a boy staring from the doorway."

"Uh, sorry about that." *Crap.* "I was desperate to see Dr. Habibah. I just found out about you and started having nightmares and weird visions and needed to see her."

Nori turns her body to face me. Her knees touch my thigh and my heart drops into my stomach. "You know what's weird about that? I had what they called an *episode* right after I saw you. The room was flashing and I jumped off the bed. Dr. Habibah basically caught me. I started yelling "Damon! Damon!" and then the room stopped flashing. I didn't even know who you were yet."

"Wow. What did Dr. Habibah say?"

"She said I must've heard your name when she was talking to you in the hallway right before my *episode*. I swear Damon, I didn't hear anything while she was out there. Dr. Habibah explained what happened to you a year ago and of course I knew our stories were connected, but I was so scared. That's why I was terrified when you wanted to meet with me."

"Are you glad you did though?"

"Very much so."

We have another lingering moment where our gazes freeze in time. Nori again jerks back toward the notebook and writes down Trevoc Hospital Workers under the *Who?* list. "I'm sure more ideas will come to us as we investigate, but this is a better plan than just going there and not knowing what to do."

"You know what? We could also talk to Dr. Habibah. She is a strong link between the two of us and would have information about both of our cases that might help."

"I didn't even think about her!" Nori scribbles down our psychologist and closes her notebook.

"Fall Break is next month so maybe we can go to Trevoc during that weekend to start investigating. I know I've been in the dark much longer than you, but we can wait a few more weeks so we don't miss school."

"Oh yeah. Good idea."

Nori smiles at me and the heart that was in my stomach has now melted. I stand up and push my chair under to divert her attention from my dopey face. "Let's try to call Dr. Habibah tonight. Maybe we can meet with her before going to Trevoc."

"Sweet."

VII

The next six weeks dragged. Long, boring lectures. Tedious tests. Football games I refused to attend despite Renner's attempt to guilt me into social activities.

I thought Nori's transition to Nomad would be difficult, but she's taking it all in stride. The counselors at school thought it would be a good idea to assign her locker near mine. I guess they figured amnesic kids gotta stick together. It's nice though.

The past few weeks, I've been able to witness Nori's social strengths. She's successfully made friends with someone from each faction. She's inclusive without being exclusive. At the home, she's excellent with the littles. She's patient, kind, and wise. Nori is equal parts compassion and bravery. We haven't had a lot of alone time because of our jam-packed schedules. To my relief, Fall Break has arrived.

We didn't want to miss any school trying to get to Trevoc, I only regret that we couldn't save more for higher quality transit. We bought bus tickets when they were cheapest we could afford. We used the money I earned from random sessions of Molecular

Biology tutoring and from Nori watching the home for Miss Elle a few times while she went out to get her hair done or to grocery shop.

We tried to contact Dr. Habibah multiple times before this trip, but her phone keeps going to a voicemail that states she is dealing with a family emergency. The message provides a number to call if another psychologist is needed and ends with a hopeless beep.

So much for that idea.

The bus ride is bumpy and smells like a mix of curry and sweaty socks. Our bus driver, Mr. Mood, assured us we'd have a smooth, comfortable ride today. Apparently, he's paid to lie to people.

Our seats are close together, but I don't mind; Nori's arm keeps brushing against mine. Despite our layers of clothing, I still feel electricity between us when we touch. I try to distract my brain from the smell of the bus and the pretty girl sitting next to me. My mind doesn't have a ton to draw from considering my circumstances, but I think about a time about two weeks ago where I woke up in the middle of the night from a nightmare so I went to the kitchen. When I walked in, Nori was standing in the dark, staring into the fridge.

"Oh! I was just going getting some water." I flick the light on.

"Sorry if I scared you. I had a dream I went strawberry picking and I wanted to see if we have any. It's my favorite fruit. And in case you are wondering, we don't have any." She shuts the fridge and hangs her head.

I go to the fridge and pour myself a glass of water. "Dissociative amnesia is weird."

"Seriously. I can't remember specific memories, but I know for sure I do not like country music."

Water almost came out of my nose. "Really? Okay, here's a strange one for you. Can someone tell me why I know the entire Time Warp *dance?"*

Nori snorts in laughter, but immediately muffles it.

"That's the real reason I don't like going to football games. Whenever the marching band plays that song in the stands. Yeah..."

She slaps her hands over her mouth mid-squeal. I use the collar of my shirt to hold in my laughter.

We jump at the sudden presence of Renner in the doorway of the kitchen. He's yawning and rubbing his eyes so I think he may have missed our conversation.

"What are you guys doing up so late?"

"Getting water."

"Uh, sleep walking?"

Renner stares at us slitty-eyed. "Okay. Um, I'm going back to bed."

"I probably should too. Goodnight boys." Nori leaves and I'm sad that our rare encounter is over.

The bus hits a pothole and sends me back to the present. The sun shines across the cornfields as the bus heads toward what feels like destiny. I'm hopeful we'll gain some new information, but deep in the pit of my stomach, my nerves are twitchy.

Suddenly, a loud banging sounds at the front of the bus and we pull over to the right shoulder. Mr. Mood checks to see if his passengers are all right and then exits the bus. The jolt caused everyone on the bus to hold their breath for a bit, but now there's nervous chatter and babies crying. The toddler in the front is crying as if they just watched someone kick their puppy. The baby in the back is screaming so loud it's reminiscent of the banshee I heard in a movie once.

Nori looks at the babies with compassion and kindness.

To me, it's all very annoying.

Time is passing and the driver still hasn't gotten back on the bus.

If I were him, I wouldn't.

Since the stop, the air has grown thick and the original bus smell has transformed into a mix of body odor, baby wipes, and humidity. Despite the smell, the driver gets back on the bus. He speaks into his microphone. "Folks, this is your driver, Mr. Mood. Sorry for the delay. A raccoon got sucked into the serpentine belt, broke it, and is now stuck in the engine. The raccoon did not make it and unfortunately, neither did a few of our cylinders. I've called for a tow truck, but it won't arrive until tomorrow morning." The bus grows loud with anguish. "But," Mr. Mood raises his voice over the chatter, "I've called for a replacement bus and it will arrive in a few hours." The other passengers cheer.

Nori looks over at me with her pleading brown eyes. "What are we going to do now? The precinct in Trevoc closes its doors in two hours and we still have 65 miles to go."

"Well, we could always hitchhike—"

"Brilliant!" Nori pops up out of her seat and starts down the aisle. I stand and grab her shoulder. I pull her close so the other passengers don't hear.

"Are you serious?"

"Yeah! We can't chance waiting for the other bus. What a waste of time and money."

It's astonishing how she can take my joke and throw logic into it.

We reach the front and Mr. Mood stands taller than I recall. "Where are you kids going?"

"To get some air. Have you smelled it back there?" I try to joke with the gentlemen but his face remains stern.

"Mr. Mood." She's so sweet it's almost gross. "I would really appreciate if we could stretch our legs for a few minutes."

"I don't know, you guys are young and I don't want anything to happen—"

Mr. Mood is interrupted by the most disgusting noise I've ever heard followed by the most putrid smell. I instinctively turn to look, though now I wish my instincts would fail once and a while. The screaming banshee baby in the back has given the bus a projectile present. Mr. Mood grabs a roll of paper towels and spray, pushes through Nori and I, grumbling on the way about how he doesn't get paid enough.

I look back at Nori. She shrugs and exits the bus and I follow close behind.

We stand a few feet behind the bus, unsure of what exactly to do.

"Maybe you should show some leg or something."

"Damon!" She smacks me on the arm and laughs. She stretches a thumb out along the highway, her flaming hair floating around as cars fly past.

"What? That's what they do in cartoons and movies!"

"Well we aren't in a cartoon so let's just focus on the task. A new way to get us to Trevoc."

"Right. This one looks promising." A little red hatchback squeals up. We duck down to look through the window. A middle-aged man donning aviators, a mullet, and western style mustache rolls the passenger side window down. He sits in the lane, far from where we are standing, so I only get a glimpse of his dingy off-white t-shirt with the sleeve pulled up to show off his "I Love Dad" tattoo.

I wish I could see his eyes, I feel like I'd be able to read him better.

"Need a lift?" His voice is raspy and deep like he's been smoking a pack a day since birth.

"Yes, sir. We're headed to Trevoc. Could you take us there?" Nori is so polite. I'm still suspicious.

"Sure. I'm goin' past Trevoc on my way to indulge myself in Reeb, a town about 20 miles past there. Hop in."

I open the passenger door for Nori. I did a quick evaluation of the car and decided that the most reliable seat this tin can offers is the front because it has a seatbelt and possibly air bags. I wouldn't necessarily deem it safe considering we don't know this man from Adam, but I want Nori to be protected from an accident. I get in the back and notice that the seat belts have all been cut and there's a swampy smell radiating from the floor. I can't imagine the places this car has been. I may not want to either.

Our mystery driver asks if he can turn on some music and we oblige. Expecting country western, my ears are ambushed with the screams of heavy metal. This is going to be worse than the broke down bus full of screaming, germ-infested children.

We get about ten miles down the road when Nori turns toward me with a slight panic in her eyes. I furrow my brow in confusion. She responds by widening her eyes. I shake my head slightly to let her know I'm not picking up on her cues. She darts her eyes quickly with a nod down toward our mystery driver's torso. I lean forward and see it. My eyes linger a little too long and I slide back into my seat. My eyes squeeze closed. The sight is burned into my brain.

Our mystery driver is taking us to our destination pantless.

He isn't naked, but the alternative isn't much better. He's wearing silky boxer shorts with the Lucky Charms leprechaun saying, "They're magically delicious!" Nori turns to face the window. As the trees whiz past, I notice her face turn shades of red, lips twist into a tight smile, body shakes, and little tears escape her eyes as she stifles a laugh.

After an excruciatingly awkward hour in the car, our bare-legged cabbie drops us off in Trevoc Square in front of the precinct and continues his journey. Nori and I lose it as soon as he drives away.

"That was probably the funniest thing I never want to see again," Nori snorts with amusement.

"I'm just glad he wasn't a serial killer! I felt weird about you sitting up front, but I do have a pen in my pocket..."

Nori stares at me, confused.

"...if push came to shove, I would've figured something out."

We burst into laughter again, needing to sit on the nearest

bench to catch our breath. Imagining me trying to take down a full-grown man with a ballpoint pen is hysterical.

After a few deep breaths and spurts of giggles, we calm ourselves down. "Okay. We need to go in before we lose more daylight."

"Right." Nori takes deep breaths, trying to regain total composure.

The precinct looks older than I remember, but my memories are from the middle of the night. We walk in the door and the room is bustling with officers. Nori approaches a policeman at his desk and asks if Officer Dennis still worked there. He tells us Dennis was promoted to private investigator and took a case outside of the state last month.

"Could we get our case files? Hers are fairly new, but mine are from a year ago."

"I need to see your Social Security cards."

Having dissociative amnesia sucks.

"Unfortunately, sir, we don't have them. We can't remember who we are. We don't have any records like birth certificates, social security cards, fingerprints, or even DNA matches."

"I'm sorry kids, juvenile records are sealed and can be retrieved if victims have proper identifi—"

"Wait!" A young officer a few desks back stands up. He squints at us as he approaches and then nods. "I'll take care of these two, Sherriff."

The deputy leads the way and motions to the seats in front of his desk. We sit and the officer smiles. "I remember you two."

"You do?" Nori grabs and squeezes my arm with excitement.

The officer chuckles, "It's pretty rare to be the officer who fails to take fingerprints off a trespassing teenager. It's especially rare to be the officer who failed twice."

"I remember you! Officer Itati!" Nori releases her grip, reaches across the table, and shakes his hand.

So polite.

I shake his hand. "Sorry we gave you such trouble."

"Oh please. We see weird things all the time. It was just late and I thought you guys were messing with me."

We laugh awkwardly.

"When you left the precinct a year ago Damon, I started researching the treatment of unidentified living persons. I found that an organization called NamUs had an online database for records of unidentifiable or missing persons. I decided to put your case information into the database in case your family tried to search for you online. I did the same thing when you were found, Nori." He types on his computer and the hope in my belly grows. "By law, the police cannot give you your juvenile records without a proper ID but because I entered your cases into the system, you can read it for yourselves."

He turns the screen towards us. "Damon, this is the record I put in for you. Nori, I opened another tab for you. I'm going to get some coffee. Let me know if there's anything else I can do for you."

I'm so engrossed in reading my case information that I don't even respond to the deputy. Nori must be too because she sits next to me, silent, focused on the screen.

UNIDENTIFIED PERSON: Living. Male.

DATE FOUND: September 5, 2016.

LOCATION: Trevoc.

The circumstances of my recovery say I was found inside an abandoned residential home in Trevoc at 11:11pm. Anyone with information concerning this male should contact the Trevoc Police Department. The hope in my belly dissipates.

"Let's try yours, Nori."

I close my tab and read Nori's case file.

UNIDENTIFIED PERSON: Living. Female.

DATE FOUND: September 5, 2017.

LOCATION: Trevoc.

Her recovery circumstances are similar other than that she was picked up outside of the residence and that she was found at 4:00pm. Nori looks at me. Her brown eyes fade with despair.

Deputy Itati sits back down at the desk, a fragrant cup of coffee in hand. "Find anything?"

"No. Nothing new anyway." I give the officer a weak smile.

"That's disappointing. I'm sorry there isn't more I could do for you kids."

Nori stands. "Thanks, Officer Itati. I think I know someone at the hospital who can help us."

We exit the precinct and head north toward the hospital. This town is much bigger than Nomad. Chain restaurants line the main strip. Commercial grocery stores, pharmacies, and gas stations are open on every corner. The intersections are at least triple the length of those back in our village. The air is loud with sounds of the expressway.

I'm a little wary about going back to the hospital after the episode I had last visit. Nori seems determined and marches right through the automatic doors and up to the same rude nurse who was there a month ago. Unexpectedly, Nori rounds the desk and gives that nurse a huge hug. "Honey! What are you doing here? I'd be far away from here if I was you!"

Nori squeezes the shoulders of the broad nurse. "Girl, you know I can't go anywhere without a Nan hug!" They embrace again, the quietness of the lobby shattered by their echoing laughter. "Nan, this is Damon."

She turns to me, throws a hand on her hip and cocks her head sideways a bit. "Oh. I know who he is. He snuck down the hospital hallway when I wasn't looking."

"Nice to–uh, meet you officially?" Nan looks like she could put me in a semi-permanent room in this place.

"Nan. We need your help."

She grabs Nori and pulls her into her bosom. "You know I'll help you. It's the nerdy one I'm not sure about."

I look down and remember I'm wearing a D20 dice sweatshirt I bought at a gaming convention I went to last winter. I glance back up and shrug. Can't deny my nerdiness wearing this.

"We need our hospital records. Mine from last week and Damon's from a year ago."

Nan scans me with her fidgeting eyes. "Anything for you my sweet girl. I have some paperwork for you to fill out, but otherwise, it should be a piece of double chocolate cake."

"My favorite!" I break their bonding time with my joke, but no one laughs. I stuff my hands into my pockets and shuffle my feet, still feeling their stares. After an inconclusive amount of time, the girls turn to each other and have a good laugh at my expense. Nan throws her arm around Nori and walks toward the back of the hospital. I quicken my pace to keep up with the girls.

We reach a lone computer near a quiet nurse's station and Nan clicks on the keys with her bright pink nails to print a few papers out. She puts the papers on two clipboards and instructs us to fill them out to retrieve our medical records.

We sit in a small lobby off the hallway and read. Name. Date of birth. Social security number. Date(s) of service.

"Nori, as much as I think Nan wants to help us, I don't think she can. I can't even fill in the spot for *name* without feeling like I'm committing fraud."

Nori takes my clipboard and brings it to Nan. I can't hear their conversation, but eventually Nan throws up an index finger, jumps onto the computer, and clicks away. I wait as Nori looks over Nan's shoulder and points to the screen illuminating their faces.

Nori signals and I amble up to the desk. "Nan remembered that unidentified persons have pre-assigned hospital numbers. She pulled yours up first."

Nori walks back to the small lobby and waits in the dark. I know I'm advanced in the sciences, but not in reading medical jargon. I stare at the page, trying to figure out what it says.

"What do you want to know deary?" I think she could sense my confusion.

"Did the doctors find any suspicious marks? Did any of the tests they ran come back with abnormal results? Did the doctors find anyone else's DNA on me?"

Nan scrolls and clicks through the program like lightning. "No strange marks or bruises and none of your tests came back with any red flags. No other DNA except your own was present. The only thing notable was that dissociative amnesia was added to the record by Dr. Maram Habibah a week after you were admitted."

"Yeah. I already knew all of that."

"Sorry sweetie. Go get Nori while I pull up her records."

I go back into the shadowy lobby and tell Nori she's next. Her hair shines like a ruby in the glow of the screen. She pulls hair behind her ears as she leans forward to inspect her records closer. They talk for a bit and then I see a single tear roll down Nori's cheek. Nan wipes it away without a word.

This is the worst.

I get up, shuffle behind the desk, and embrace Nori. I stare into Nan's hurt eyes. "Nan, thank you for helping us. We probably wouldn't have had anything to look at if it weren't for you."

Nori turns and gives Nan a goodbye hug. I take her under my

arm and we walk out of the hospital and back toward the bus stop. Dark clouds loom overhead. I pray deep inside that the rain holds until we get home.

The bus ride back was quiet. Our leads were dead ends and that is devastating. Nori eventually told me on the bus that her records were clear and all her tests came back negative, including the rape kit. While she is relieved about that, she, like me, hoped the records would have something else for us to investigate. We need to go back to the drawing board for ideas, but I think we'll take a break for a little while. Recovering from this rejection could take a while. As soon as we stepped on the porch at the children's home, the bottom fell out of the sky. Giant raindrops and pea-sized hail pummel the ground.

I'm thankful my prayers were answered in this instance. Perhaps I should pray harder for an answer to the mystery of our lives.

VIII

I stare at the bed slats above me, and try to figure out what happened. I've been staring at these same slats every day for a year. They don't bring any more answers than they did before we got our newest resident to the children's home.

The bunk shakes as Renner's head appears off the edge. I turn toward the wall.

"Psst."

"Renner, go back to sleep. It's Sunday," I whisper since the other boys are still asleep.

"Psssst."

I let out a low growl, like a dog guarding a bone, except I guard my sanity.

SMACK!

Something hits my hip and flips into the space in front of my torso. I put my hand down from under my chin to feel around. Tablet.

"Just read it."

The screen shines bright with an article I'm all too familiar with, "Amnesic Boy Found in Trevoc."

"I've read this a thousand times." I roll my eyes and put the tablet down.

"Read it again." Renner pulls himself back up to his pillow, the creaking bunk echoing against the high ceiling.

I could say I read it and don't but then I wouldn't hear the end of it from Renner. I take a big sigh and read over the article again. It turns out the article is just a screenshot and Renner underlined the address of the house. I click the screen black.

I never thought to go back there.

A murmur from above breaks the silence. "I know. I'm a freaking genius."

🕐🕑🕒🕓🕔

Monday, October 23, 2017

Nori, Renner, and I are early to first hour and Mr. Bard isn't around. Nori leans over my shoulder and Renner pulls his chair into the aisle. "Did you find it?"

"The internet is super slow, so no. Not yet." I'm trying to search for the abandoned house through a mapping website on a class laptop. After a few impatient minutes, the page refreshes and there it is. 1111 Levart Circle. I think the house has white siding, but it's hard to tell because of the small picture and the dingy color. This rancher is our next stop.

"We can't just show up. You were tackled to the ground."

"Nori, it was nighttime and they thought I was a vandal. We'll go during the day."

"Maybe you can get an escort. If you tell the police the reason you are there, maybe they can go with you and then they won't arrest you for trespassing."

Nori and I exchange a look of interest. Renner shakes his head. "You guys act like I never have good ideas," Renner says as Mr. Bard walks in, "but everyone knows I'm the brains of this operation."

Mr. Bard bursts into laughter on the way to the lab closet. "I don't know the context of this conversation, but that last bit didn't sound quite right."

Nori and I laugh and Renner tries to act embarrassed, despite the smile creeping up the corner of his mouth. Sometimes teachers surprise me. It's like they are regular humans too.

🕐🕑🕓🕕🕖

A fter an interesting lesson on recombinant plasmids, the bell sounds to end the hour. Nori stands up, grabs her coat, and slings it around her. A metal clanging interrupts the sound of shuffling students. Those still in the room look around, confused by the sound, but are only deterred for a moment before continuing out the door. Nori's eyes widen with panic as she puts her hands in her pockets. Color leaves her face. Frantically, she feels around all her pockets, inside and outside, coat and pants. She looks back up at me with absolute desperation. "Help me!"

"Huh?"

"I lost my pocket watch!"

That must be the sound we heard. Kinda strange for a girl to have a pocket watch, but whatever floats her boat. I search the floor near our desks and Nori spans out toward the back of the classroom. Renner joins in without question, checking in front of Mr. Bard's counter. Mr. Bard himself pops out of the equipment closet and stares at his students sprawled out on the floor. "What are we looking for?"

"Pocket watch!" Nori yells from under a counter.

Mr. Bard nods and scans the floor. I pull the front door away from the wall to check behind and there it is, a silver pocket watch. Purple light escapes the seam of the cover. I kneel to pick it up and it happens again. The light flickers, and my vision is interrupted.

I'm back in the abandoned house. There's no mistaking that this is the night I woke up. I'm looking toward the front door and out of the corner of my left eye I see a purple glow. I feel a small hand on my shoulder and a voice. My vision strobes and I'm back on the floor of the science room. Nori shrieks with delight. "You found it!"

Before I can grab it, Nori snatches it and stuffs it into her coat pocket. I'm not even standing when Nori says a quick thanks and runs out the door.

"Doe. Emit. Do you need passes to your next class?"

"Thanks, Mr. Bard. That would be great."

Waiting for our passes, Renner gives me a puzzled expression and I shrug. That was too familiar. Where did that watch come from and why didn't I know about it until now?

🕐🕑🕒🕓🕔

I meet up with Renner and Nori at lunch and there's no mention of the watch incident during first hour. I'm starting to notice how often she reaches into her pocket where she safeguards the timepiece.

Thinking back, there were quite a few times where she would reach into her jacket. I always thought it was a nervous habit. Now I'm wondering what that watch is all about.

Renner isn't talking much while we eat. He's deep into *Walden*. When things are bothering him, he dives into that book. I'd check to see what's going on, but I feel like it should be a man-to-man conversation, or rather, a man-to-nerd conversation.

Nori and I are trying to figure out how and when we can get

back to Trevoc to visit the house. Thanksgiving is in a few weeks. I know it'll be busy at the children's home since Miss Elle puts on a big feast for the house, but maybe this holiday, she'll be happier with a few less teens to entertain. Travel costs are cheaper on actual holidays. Makes logical sense. Nori is on board. I think Renner is going to join us this time, but it's hard to tell if he's nodding at his book or at our plans. If he does come, it'll be interesting to get his insight.

🕐🕑🕒🕓🕔

"I'm really glad you're going with us this time."

"Whatever." His arrow whistles through the air, striking just outside of center.

"You've been in a funk today."

Renner loads another arrow and takes aim. "Don't worry about it. You have enough on your plate."

The pit in my stomach echoes with guilt. I'm so wrapped up in my own problems that I've neglected my friend again.

"I'd appreciate a break from my stuff."

He shoots and then rests his bow on the ground. "My grand-mother passed away on Thanksgiving."

I trace the lines on my hand. "I forgot. I'm sorry."

"I've mourned her death and accepted she's gone, but what bothers me is that I'm having a hard time remembering her. I used to think of her and immediately, I'd see her face. Hear her voice. The older I get, the harder it is to remember. The best I have now is the book. She wrote little notes about Thoreau's theories or reminders that my parents would come back for me. Sometimes, the pages still smell like her perfume. Her handwriting and her scent are the only hints of family I have left. I guess it just hit me harder today than usual."

No wonder he treats that book like gold. I purse my lips, unable to form words.

"I guess that's why I want to help you and Nori. You have family out there, somewhere, and I want to help you remember them."

Best friends are hard to come by, even when you have all your memories. I'm glad I have Renner. He's as loyal and trustworthy as it gets.

🕐🕑🕒🕓🕔

Thursday, November 23, 2017

G ravy is the best smell of all the smells. I could probably just drink gravy on its own, but that's frowned upon. You gotta put meat juice on meat, not just straight into your belly. Pretty much everything Miss Elle is making in the kitchen smells like heaven. Except for the Brussels sprouts. Those smell like feet.

It's amazing how she works during holidays like these. Though she starts early, sometimes 3 or 4 in the morning, she's quiet, like a cooking ninja. She moves with purpose around the cabinets. Her recipes all lined up. Every utensil and ingredient ready in the order she needs them. Part of me is bummed I'm going to miss out on this meal. The other part of me will be glad the chaos will be 90 miles behind us.

I tie my shoes and zip up my coat. I peak into Renner's bed. He's still sleeping. I shake him a little and then take a few steps back. He tends to swing if I scare him awake. I'm not repeating that mistake again.

A scratchy voice answers, "What?"

"Renner, it's Thanksgiving." I'm trying to whisper to keep the other boys from waking up, but I'm still a few steps back just in case he decides to throw a left hook anyway. "We need to get to the bus station."

He replies with a series of deep, wet coughs. Rolling over, I notice his face is sweaty and pale. "I'm not going to make it today. Must've caught something at school."

I open my mouth to offer condolences, but he's fast asleep again. I was really hoping to get Renner's thoughts on this trip, but Nori and I can handle it.

I shut the door and head to the kitchen. Nori is at the table eating a biscuit with a little turkey and gravy on it. *Yum.* Viv is creeping through kitchen from the couch room, but Miss Elle turns on a dime and shoos the hungry creature away. I walk up to Miss Elle as she stirs something on the stove. She gets on her tippy toes so I can give her a proper kiss on the cheek. "I'm going to miss you today, but I understand. Where's Renner?"

"He's caught something pretty nasty, Miss Elle. You might want to quarantine him so he doesn't get the whole house sick like last year when Asa brought home the stomach flu." I walk to Nori and sit down next to her. "It was like an exorcism gone wrong in this place."

Miss Elle glances up at the chicken clock ticking on the wall. "You two better get on your way. I'm praying your bus doesn't have raccoon troubles again."

"You and me both, Miss Elle." Nori laughs.

🕐🕑🕒🕓🕔

Choosing a holiday to take our trip back to Trevoc may have helped our wallets, but not with the quest. The Police Department is short staffed and need to focus their energies on emergencies, not a couple of punk kids trying to go see an abandoned old house. They gave permission look around, but forbade us to go inside. The officer pointed us in the right direction and a few miles later we arrive.

"The satellite image must be old. This place is a hole." The dingy white house we saw online is a palace compared to the dilapidated structure before us. The yard is about a foot tall, overgrown with twisted weeds and thorns. A sad lamp post sits in the yard, flickering with an orange light. The rusted railing near the front door is wrapped with police tape with the words DO NOT CROSS blocking the entrance. The worst of it is the front of the house. Hit hard with graffiti, the most prominent words, HOME WRECKERS, stretch the length of the house. The sight hits the pit of my stomach like a rogue anchor.

Nori starts down the front walk and I grab her arm. "What are you doing?"

"Hey, the cop said we couldn't go in. He didn't say we couldn't look around the *outside*." I let go and allow her to continue toward the house. I'd never admit this to her face, but she's the brave one of the two of us.

She puts her hands up to the front window to shade the reflection of the overcast clouds. Curtains block her attempt. She continues down the right side of the house, passing the giant words that still grip me. She stops and runs her fingers along the final S. She yells to me, "It's dry. Must've been a long time ago." She rounds the corner and I am left very aware of my solitude. I finally give in and run up the front sidewalk, around the side of the house.

When I reach Nori in the backyard. It's astonishing in the worst way possible. The front might be a street artists' dream, but the back is a scene from a horror movie. It's unbelievable that it's still standing considering there is nothing holding up the back of the house. The siding peels away from the center and the walls are gone. The furniture up against that once existing wall are blackened. I bet if I touched something, it would crumble into a pile of dust like in a cartoon. Everything in view is covered in what looks like snow, but upon closer examination, it's ash. I pinch some off the ground near me and roll the ash between my fingers and thumb. It's gritty and crumbling. It seems the fire happened long ago, despite the still strong stench of char and rot.

Did I just rub someone's remains into my skin?

My stomach turns.

Our feet are frozen, taking in the sights and smells of the fire-consumed house. Nori broke the silence. "The night I was found, I smelled mildew and char. Now I know why."

I nod, unable to form words in my dry mouth.

Nori takes the first step and I follow her around the right side of the house. She stops and I run into the back of her. There's a little old lady standing on the sidewalk in front of the house. She's short and frail. Her head is decorated with a shower cap, curlers of thin hair stuffed underneath. Her fluffy pink robe drags the ground and her bunny slippers poke out from the bottom. She wiggles a slender finger back and forth to signal for our approach. Though the anchor in my stomach just got heavier, I'm not letting Nori lead anymore. I take her hand and pull ahead of her. When we get closer, I see countless age spots covering her face and chest. If the wrinkles on her skin were any indication of her age, I'd say she's as old as time itself. She reaches into a fuzzy pocket and pops her teeth. I try to make my shutter of disgust unde-tectable. "What are you two doing out here on Thanksgiving?" Her voice is quiet, slow, and warbled.

Nori speaks up before I have the chance. "We were thinking about buying this home. It definitely doesn't match the picture we saw online, does it honey?" She squeezes my hand. She looks up at me and bats her eyelashes in an exaggerated attempt to fool this lady.

"No, it sure doesn't. Do you know what happened to this house, ma'am?"

The elder sucks her teeth a little. The sound makes my stomach curdle. "A fire claimed this home years ago."

"Do you know who lived here? It was unclear on the ad and our agent has no information either." Nori tries to keep cool, but the sound of hope rises in her voice.

"There was once a couple who lived here. A newly-wed couple. They had a baby, but a year later the father skipped town. The town had a field day with that one. I figured he ran out because he couldn't take the pressures of fatherhood. Another year passed, and the wife ran out too, leaving the baby behind. A few years later, the caretaker started a fire in that home. She couldn't take the pressure of taking care of a child that was the talk of the town anyways. I think at the last minute she decided she couldn't take her life and the life of the child so she ran out of the inferno just as quick as she could. She died, but the child lived. The state took him away. No one has been back to this house since, well, until they found you two in there."

Our eyes grow wide.

"Don't you think I'd recognize the biggest gossip this town has heard since this house fire? Two kids, found in the same abandoned house with amnesia? Ha! It was so juicy I had to take my teeth out for a week!" She pops her teeth out and cackles like a witch.

Nori grabs my hand. Trying to keep my voice even I ask her one last question, "Ma'am, do you know the name of the couple that once lived here?"

She stops cackling long enough to throw her teeth back in. She scratches her cheek and squints her eyes. "The old noodle's been failing me with the real doozies. Sorry kids. I wish I could help you more."

Nori releases her grip on my hand. I guess she was hoping for more too.

"Thank you for your time."

At first the old woman shuffles away but then she whips her body around so fast it causes Nori to gasp with surprise. Her nimble fingers wrap around my wrist. She pulls me so we are eye to eye. She lets loose a dry cough. "Emit. Their last name was Emit."

My heart stops. "Do you know how they spelled it?"

The old lady releases my wrist to pick a finger between her curlers. "I can picture it on their mailbox. It was E-M-I-T."

I feel my hand tightening around Nori's, but I can't stop it.

"Damon, what's wrong?" Her emerald eyes swell with concern.

I can't breathe.

"Emit is Renner's last name."

IX

Normally, when you close your eyes, you see darkness.

When I close mine, all I see is red.

My new friends, Betrayal and Bitterness, kick me in the chest. One word pierces my lungs.

Emit.

Breathing is more difficult than I remember. The knot in my chest loosened, but I don't know what to do with the ends. My heart pounds slow but hard and angry from shock. For the sake of life, it needs time to calm down.

Emit.

My eyes are heavy with exhaustion and I feel lightheaded. My body pumped with anger for so long, it leaked out of my ears leaving a void for confusion and anxiety to fill.

Emit.

It echoes in the empty shell that was once me. Processing this small bit of information is almost impossible. It snuck up on me, disguised in a robe and false teeth.

Emit.

🕐🕑🕒🕓🕔

This bus ride is more than I can bear. How could the person I trust most have anything to do with the disappearance of my memories? My life? It's ignorant to jump to conclusions without knowing all the facts. It's ill advised to be angry about something with unclear details. At least that's what Nori has been trying to convince me of since we left Trevoc.

Easier said than done.

I'm a freight train with no breaks, the stoker of my hatred shoveling more coal into the firebox with no chance of slowing down. Nori looks at me with concern and sadness. She can't possibly experience this news the way I am. She's new to amnesic life, dealing with it for mere months. The connections between my actual life and the life I live now have been severed for over a year. I wander blindly through a life that isn't mine with someone who is supposed to be my best friend.

Maybe he kept me close so I wouldn't suspect anything. Keep your friends close, but your enemies in the bunk beneath you.

The bus drops us off. Everything is numb. We walk up to the children's home and there he is. Sitting in a rocking chair, wrapped in a blanket. I take the two steps up to the porch. He stands and walks toward me with a weary smile on his face.

"How did she die, Renner?"

He squints at me and coughs. "What?"

"Your grandmother. How did she die?"

He shakes his head. "Smoke inhalation. The house caught fire. She had just enough time to grab me and *Walden*."

My right fist connects with his left eye, quickly and swiftly. Nori yells out. Renner hits the ground, holding his face.

I continue through the front door, straight to my bed, knuckles pounding and bloody.

"**D**amon, this is Miss Elle. She runs the Pilut Children's Home where you will be staying." Dr. Habibah moves out of the way so we can shake hands. She leads us down the walkway, up the porch steps, and into the front entrance of the home. She talks to me about the house, but the sounds are muffled by the thoughts firing in my brain. She leads me to the boys' quarters. The boys in the room sit up from their bunks and stare. My heart races, my breathing quickens. I'm finding that being in the spotlight causes me quite a bit of anxiety.

Dr. Habibah tells me that it's normal, but I don't want it to be. I want to know who I am and what happened to me.

Dr. Habibah says goodnight and leaves me in the boys' quarters. I walk toward the back of the room and see a guy, about my age, sitting on the bottom bunk. His jacket is zipped up to his neck with the collar popped up. He's unlacing his combat boots from beneath his dark jeans. The boy looks up at me. At first glance, he's quite intimidating. He stands and his tall stature adds more threat to his image. But then he does something that seems out of the ordinary, considering his demeanor. He smiles.

"Hi, I'm Renner."

"Um. Hi. I'm Damon. Or at least I am now."

His eyes widen and his brow furrows. He shakes his head back and forth as if he's erasing a drawing from an etch-a-sketch board. "Damon, that sounds weird and complicated."

"It is."

He laughs and it puts me at ease. "You can have this bunk. I've been wanting to switch to the top for a while, but haven't had a reason to." Renner pulls off his boots and climbs to the top.

"Thanks. Hey, Renner right?"

He hangs his head off the bed so his dark hair looks like it's sticking straight up. "Yeah?"

"How long have you been here?"

"Twelve years."

Wow. I know given my situation I shouldn't trust anyone, but Renner seems like someone I could grow to be friends with. "Bummer."

"Yep. We'll talk more in the morning."

"Okay."

"And Damon..."

"WHAT THE HELL WAS THAT FOR?"

The yelling shakes me awake. Renner stands near the bed, a shiner growing under his left eye. He sniffles and coughs, still sick from this morning. The rage that overcame me this morning returns. My jaw clenches, my fists are tight. I'd take a swing at him again if the other boys weren't watching. I get out of bed, and stand chest to chest with Renner.

"Boys, get out." Without hesitation the boys jump up, help the younger ones, and close the door behind them. "That was for lying to me."

"What are you talking about?"

"You know."

"If I knew, I'd probably understand why I got sucker punched in the face. Right now, I just want to return the favor."

"Your family was involved in my abduction. In Nori's abduction."

His demeanor changes in an instant. His face softens, his shoulders drop, and his eyes fill with concern. He takes a step back as if this news is surprising. "What?"

"At the abandoned house, we met a neighbor. She described a couple that abandoned their child to a caretaker, but she died from a fire and the baby was taken away. Renner, we saw the back of the house. It was scorched."

Renner searches the floor with his eyes, darting from object to object. *What an actor.* "Don't you think it's coincidental you woke up in my childhood home?"

"Not when this *entire time* you've told me that your grandmother promised your parents would return."

My patience is thin.

Renner is looking angry again. His neck stiffens and his words are short and loud out of his tight lips. "You think my parents abducted you and Nori *instead of* coming back for *their own son*?"

"That's exactly what I think."

"You're an idiot, Damon. So desperate for information about your past, you're willing to ruin a friendship to cling to something you heard from a nosy neighbor."

"Pretty much."

He steps back up to me so our chests meet again. He looks down and his dark eyes rage. I keep my body tense, ready for a blow in any direction. Instead, Renner huffs, turns around, and storms out of the room.

I know his parents did this.

I'm going to prove it.

🕐🕑🕒🕓🕔

Saturday, November 26, 2017

The library is quiet on this Saturday afternoon. Snow falls behind the towering stained-glass windows in front of us. The library is empty, besides our favorite stuck-up librarian and us. The temperature of the room matches the temperature outside so Nori and I sit close as we burn out the search engine.

We search the name Emit and wait. The results are several links to dictionary definitions on the verb emit. The links that follow are no more helpful, just random technology and engineering companies. Nori takes over the keyboard, typing the phonetic pronunciation, emmitt, into the search engine. She sighs in anguish at dozens of articles discussing pro-football great Emmitt Smith. The librarian, hovering in the bookshelves near our computer, shushes Nori.

I try the address of the house. The first article is about Nori and the second about me. The third seems more promising:

FIRE SCORCHES TREVOC HOME

"A Trevoc home is nearly consumed with flames Thanksgiving evening. The fire chief tells TRE 11 that the rancher caught on fire around 7pm last night and that firefighters responded quickly, keeping the fire from spreading through the entire home.

After a thorough investigation, the town police and fire chiefs released a statement to the press:

"It is unclear what started the fire last night. An arson investigator has been contacted and will search for signs of foul play. The two residents of the home, a woman and a toddler, escaped and were treated at Trevoc Hospital. The names of the victims will not be released at this time. We can say with certainty that woman did not make it through the night and the boy only suffered superficial burns. He will be given over to next of kin or to the state if none exist. We appreciate your concern, but we believe this was an isolated accident and not a deliberate attack on our community."

According to the town bylaws, the damaged structure will remain standing until a will can be procured and a new owner pronounced. The police and fire teams ask that citizens keep a respectable distance or they will be treated as trespassers on the property."

"Nothing new here." I close the article. The librarian coughs loud, with suggestion, from a shelf behind me. I turn around and shush the old lady and she looks at me wide-eyed with shock.

Nori stifles a laugh. I look at the clock on the computer, ten minutes until they close. *What an impatient witch.*

Trying to hold back the anger escaping through my slamming fingertips, I search Renner Emit. Nothing of significance comes up except for annoying articles from the school about his college scholarship opportunities through archery.

Nothing on his family.

Nothing linking him to the fire.

"What if we try some combinations?" Nori slides her fingers to the keyboard and types Emit Trevoc. The dictionary entries pop up again as well as a tourism page for the town of Trevoc. Near the bottom of the page, a headline catches my attention. The article is brief.

PROFESSOR ABANDONS GROUNDBREAKING RESEARCH

"President Gereg of Elbissop University, Trevoc announced the end of a five-year grant under the Department of Biochemistry. Dr. Marc D. Emit, the lead research scientist for the grant, submitted in his notice of resignation, by email, to the President after having gone missing for nearly four weeks. The professor's wife, Selah, responded to our questions with a firm no comment.

The grant promised extensive research on the nervous system and its capabilities beyond the five senses. Dr. Emit boasted that his research could answer the questions often asked by Hollywood movies: does time travel exist and can it be achieved with the power of our own sensory system? Due to the controversy surrounding Dr. Emit's absence, President Gereg and the university made a strong statement by reallocating the grant money to the Department of Family Counseling to fund their research on alternative homes for orphaned children."

I try to look up Marc D. Emit, but the article that pops up is the one I just read. Selah Emit results in a contemporary Christian trio and Bible passages from Psalms and Habakkuk. Everything else is a public record search with random names and addresses across the country.

"We've learned that Renner's parents' names are Marc and Selah and that he was a professor at a university until he abandoned his research. I'm intrigued that he was studying biological processes to prove the capabilities of—"

Nori eyelids flicker, as if she'd taken a micro-nap. That's usually how others look when I discuss science with them. We've been at this for a while and the cold isn't helping. "That must be when the old lady said he abandoned the home, his wife leaving a year later."

The librarian coughs again, this time to my right. Nori leans backward and yells, "Hey! We still have 5 minutes. Don't you have a card catalog to organize or something?" The woman, visibly disturbed by Nori's outburst, walks away.

Nori leans forward with her forearms pressed against her thighs. She fiddles with her ring, turning it clockwise around her finger.

"Where did you get that ring anyway?"

"Oh this? I woke up wearing it. I never take it off. Might've been from my former life." She stops to admire the square amethyst gem and then stuffs her hands into her pockets.

She sits up. "I've got it!" She pulls out the pocket watch and hands it to me. "There has to be a connection between our abduction and this watch. It was glowing purple on the floor the night I was found. Before I left the house, I grabbed it and put it in my pocket. When they tested me at the hospital, I kept it in my sock for safekeeping. I'm not sure why I even took it. I almost completely forgot about it. I knew it was familiar, other than being

Renner's last name." She turns the pocket watch over in her hand and engraved on the back is a word I've come to loathe, *Emit*.

She slides the watch into my hands and I run my thumb across the name. Chills shoot down my spine and my breath catches. I run my fingers along the edge of the face and feel three bumps along the right side. I flip the watch over in my hand and click the bow to open the cover. Multiple dials are displayed. The first is the large, main display with Roman numerals for keeping the time. The other three dials are small, centered around the main clock hands. The left dial has the first three letters of every month around it. The top dial is numbered for the days of the month from 1 to 31, but shows odd numbers, with the even numbers represented by a dot. The right dial, where you would normally find the seconds, contains numbers starting at 1 and then counting by tens to 100. Each number is divided by a line and within each second of numbers, five little tick marks. That dial has two hands within.

"You know what I never noticed before?" Nori leans in and points to the face. "All of the hands are frozen."

I drop the watch. The action scares Nori and a little squeal escapes her mouth. As usual, the librarian's *shhhh* comes this time from the front corner of the building. My hands are shaking so bad I can't pick up the watch. Nori reaches down and whispers, "What's wrong?"

"Look where they stopped."

Nori squints her eyes and pulls the watch face close. After a few moments, the watch flings from her hands and into my lap. Her eyes are wide and her hands cover her mouth.

September 5, 2016, 11:11pm

The exact date, and time, I was found.

Monday, November 27, 2017

The warning bell rings for class to start. Mr. Bard displays the bell work question on the screen.

And I wait.

Renner walks in and it begins. Whispering. Students from all around move like a slow wave of the sea. Churning. Bubbling. Hissing. Renner gets his notebook out of his bag before he realizes the storm brewing around him. He sits still, darting his eyes to different groups of people. The whispers get louder and harsher. Renner wrinkles his brow, zips his coat up to his neck, and writes the bell work question, "How does dominance play a role in choosing a mate in the animal kingdom?"

The social seas of high school churn with laughter and disgust. Mr. Bard tries to calm the waters with humor. This diverts their conversations to written form. Papers pass around the room. One paper makes its way up to Renner's desk and before the kid beside him can get it, Renner snatches it. Large, bold words stretch across the page.

RENNER EMIT'S PARENTS ABDUCT CHILDREN.

I watch Renner's face emblaze, red cheeks, ears, and neck. His shoulders heave. The steam must've built up fast because he shoots out of his chair, grabs my collar, and yanks me to my feet. His dark eyes swirl with madness as he forces my gaze. "Did you do this?" He practically spits in my eyes, his hot breath consuming my air.

Mr. Bard, in a fit of sudden athleticism, leaps over his counter like a pommel horse and grabs Renner off me. "Mr. Emit! Go to the principal's office! NOW!" He pulls a fighting Renner to the door and slams it shut. A loud, metallic thud follows like the sound of a limb against a locker.

I straighten out my shirt, turn to my troops, and give a very large smirk. The students respond in similar fashion. I sit back down and Mr. Bard resumes class, his voice shaky from the adrenaline of that sudden outburst.

I look over at Nori. I think I may have impressed her with my latest scheme. Instead, her face is in her hands. How could she possibly be upset about this? We have no recollection of our real lives and he and his family have something to do with it. Since we can't find proof, maybe we can force it out of Renner. She knew I was going to try something to get him to confess; I just left the details vague. I came to school earlier than usual and told Hannah, Nomad High's gossip queen, that Renner's parents were involved in Nori and I's abduction. That's all I had to do. That and sit back and watch his world burn.

He deserves it if he knows *anything* about his parents or why they did this to us.

I can hear sniffles coming from Nori's direction. I can't believe she feels bad for him. She didn't know him like I did, at least how I *thought* I did.

🕐🕑🕒🕓🕔

"Nori! Nori, wait up!" I slip on some black ice, but catch my balance. I'm not sure how she moves so fast on this sidewalk, but she has a good lead on me.

"No! What you did was wrong."

"You can't be serious!" I yell down the hill to her.

She spins around like a figure skater, her auburn hair whipping around in the cold winter air. "Incredibly serious." Her dark eyes match the overcast sky and probably the misplaced disappointment she feels in me.

"It had to be done. People need to know so he will finally tell the truth."

"You didn't have to do that way, Damon. Ever since you found out the name of the homeowners and saw my stupid pocket watch, you've been a loose cannon. First you punch him, now you punish him. I feel like I don't even know you." She spins back around to continue down the path to the home.

My impatience and anger over take me. "Did you ever?" I reach out and clench her shoulder. She shoots her head toward my hand and pulls her shoulder down to free it from my grasp.

"What's that supposed to mean?"

I raise my voice, as I tower over her. "How do *you* know who I am when *I* don't even know who I am? Those monsters stole us from our homes, from our families. Whatever they did with us, or God forbid *to* us, caused us to lose our most important memories. Maybe in my past life, I was a jerk. Maybe in your past life, you weren't so self-righteous and perfect all the time. But we'll never know, will we? Not until we get answers. Are you willing to do whatever it takes to find our true selves? I am!"

It looks like lightning passing through her gaze, like a switch was flipped. She squares up to me with bravery and heat and gets right in my face. Instead of yelling, she leans in slowly and whispers in my ear.

"I may not know who you were, but I know who you are now. You are a monster."

She leans back to meet my gaze, narrows her eyes, and walks away.

If she's going to insult me, she should at least use the word correctly. If she means the noun, I'm not a creature who is large, ugly, and frightening. In fact, I'm the complete opposite. If used as a verb, to criticize severely, well, okay. *No! I'm justified in my actions.* They may not seem logical—

My vision flickers around me. I take a knee just in case this one is a doozie. My sight goes dark, but no visions appear. I hear only a woman's voice. It's oddly familiar. Older. All she says is, *"Rather than love, than money, than fame, give me truth."*

My eyes flicker, again and the village sites return to view. I stand up, my knee now soaked from the snow and ice.

I know those words. Of course, I know those words.

They are found in the next place I need to look for clues. I'm not sure how I'm going to get that book away from Renner since it's practically glued to him.

Walden Pond had answers for Thoreau. Perhaps it will have some for me.

My head is hazy after that flash. When I get back to the house, I'll sit down with Nori and try to reason with her. Try to come up with a better way to get information out of Renner.

Maybe Nori was right. Maybe I am a monster.

I continue down the sidewalk toward the porch and she's sitting in a rocking chair. I hope she is waiting to apologize because that's what I want to do. When I get up the stairs, I look up to see Renner sitting next to her. He's holding the note from class and her hand is holding his arm, her thumb stroking back and forth. Renner looks up at me surprised and Nori's head whirls around like a top. She pulls her hand away, but it's too late for that.

They stare at me. The awkwardness is thick enough to taste. I let it linger as the fury builds in my abdomen. When it feels like my insides could explode all over the porch, I turn, and walk inside. I close the door behind me.

Nori was wrong. I'm not a monster.

He is.

Soon enough, she'll see.

🕐🕑🕒🕓🕔

Monday, December 4, 2017

The office is freezing. Since 90 percent of the year consists of snow, the school has heat, but no air conditioning, except for the main office, computer labs, library, and auditorium. Mrs. Anina stands behind her desk, a guard dog between our principal and the outside world. Her arms are crossed, shoulder muscles broad and tight, and her eyes laser-focused on me. If Mrs. Anina isn't a guard dog, she's certainly a body builder.

Mr. Kilik's door opens and Hannah pops out of the room. Her eyes squint with mischief as she grins at me, like evil scientists in those old cartoons who for some reason always have a pet cat. Her steps are quick and she leaves a trail of cheap perfume in the air. Mr. Kilik calls my name and walks back into his office. I swallow hard and take a deep breath. It's been a week since the rumor caught on. After seeing Hannah's face, I have a feeling she stirred the pot a little too much this time. Mrs. Anina eventually sits in her chair, never taking her eyes off of me.

Mr. Kilik's office is small, mostly because there are floor-to-ceiling bookshelves that wrap all the way around his office. Old books. Tall books. Red books. Any book you can think of and they all have little post-it notes sticking out of the tops as if he's been doing major research. The single window in the room is behind his desk, but the glass is opaque so all you can see are shadowy figures. The room smells like rotting wood and old cigars. He tells me to close the door and have a seat.

Mr. Kilik is old. His kids are grown and have kids of their own. The combed white hair suggests years of experience and stress. His thick, round glasses enlarge the bags under his eyes. He sports a tweed coat with elbow patches and a bowtie. I don't think there's been a day since I started at this school that he hasn't worn a bowtie. When he speaks, he has a proper accent, like he was raised by the Queen of England in Middle America. I respect Mr. Kilik. He deals with teenagers and their antics daily. Anyone who willingly chooses to do this demands respect and deserves to get paid handsomely; two things I'm sure are not true of Mr. Kilik.

"Damon. I owe you an apology."

"I don't understand."

"It has come to my attention that a fellow student harassed you last week."

"Oh, that. Well—"

"I wish you had reported this to me sooner. I have a zero-tolerance policy for bullying at this school."

"Uh…" My face grows warm. What a time for irony.

"I can assure you Damon, I took care of the situation swiftly and mercilessly."

"Mr. Kilik, this is unnes—"

"Renner Emit will no longer be a problem for you at Nomad High. I rearranged his schedule, moved his locker, and removed him from extracurricular activities." He displays a proud smile as my heart drops to my stomach.

This is not going to end well for me.

"Mr. Kilik, with all due respect, while that might help me at school, I still live in the same home as him."

He makes a short *hm* sound and shrugs. "Unfortunately, I can't do anything about that. If he continues to be a threat to you outside of these walls, perhaps you should report him to the police."

I stare at him and blink a few times. My words come out slow and sticky. "Thanks Mr. Kilik. I need to get home. Have a good afternoon."

He stands up, buttons his jacket, and holds out a hand. I give a firm handshake to the old man and bolt out the door, almost running square into bulldog Mrs. Anina.

🕐🕑🕒🕓🕔

I get halfway home before I'm grabbed by the collar from behind. I lose my glasses in the jolt and I'm dragged into the alley next to the pizza place. I don't see it coming, but instead feel it in the cracking of my nose. An explosion of blood follows the blow. I cup my hand to catch the blood and look up at my blurry attacker.

Renner.

His jacket is unzipped, sleeves rolled up, eyes wild. He's seething. He pants audibly like a charging bull.

"You ruined my life, Damon."

I stand up and wring out my bloody hand. "Likewise."

Another fist connects with my left eye and I hit the ground again. A kick to the stomach knocks the wind out of me and causes me to cough. Now I know why he prefers to wear those giant boots.

"I can't believe this." He paces in front of me while I search for the air. I can feel it, but can't quite get into my lungs. "I don't know why you and Nori suddenly woke up in my childhood home and I don't know why you trust some crazy neighbor over me, but you listen to me, Damon." He delivers another kick to my gut and gets on his hands and knees to yell in my ear, "If my parents were going to come back to kidnap a child, why wouldn't it be me? Huh? Why wouldn't they just come back and get the child they abandoned?" He slams his hand down on my ear, drawing blood from both my ear and the cheek that scrapes the pavement below. "Get up!"

I manage a few sips of air and steady myself. I get on all fours, turn to sit, and lean myself up against the brick wall. Despite coughing and bleeding from multiple sites, I scowl at my former best friend.

"I've lost everything because of you. I got switched out of my classes mid-year and now I'm in organic chemistry. The teacher won't let me make up any of the assignments they've already completed. I might fail my senior year. Oh, and on top of that, they kicked me out of archery. Do you understand what you've done to me, Damon? That was my shot at college. I'm trying to get academic and archery scholarships so I can go to college and finally get away from this place." He grabs my collar, pulls me to my feet, and gets in my face. "You took everything away from me because some psychos took everything from you and Nori. Well, now I will make sure everything left in your life is taken away from you too." A left hook to my jaw knocks me back to the ground, blood splitting out of my mouth. His boots scrape the ground as he marches away.

X

I understand the science of hematology. I know how blood
flows, takes in nutrients, and transports waste. I'm fascinated
by how red blood cells deliver oxygen to the lungs and how white
blood cells fight infection. I've now learned, it tastes like metal.

After passing out in the middle of the alley, a pizza delivery
driver found me and called for help. An EMT brought me to the
Nomad ER and now I'm waiting in triage for the next available
room. A nurse has been in and out checking my vitals. He's back
to take some blood. *Haven't I lost enough of that today?*

"Your body replaces and creates new blood all the time. Quit
whining." The nurse is tall and stoic. "The EMT who found your
glasses looked in your bag for identification and called the children's home. The woman who answered said she'd be
right over."

"Miss Elle." I close my eyes. I hear a quiet knock at the door.

"That's my cue." The nurse grabs his caddy of needles and
vials and leaves. I hear feet shuffling towards me. When I open
my eyes, I immediately shut them again.

Nori.

"Miss Elle took the littles to the barber. I was running out the door before the EMT could say goodbye." Her voice is quiet, but warbles with grief. She sniffs. "I know I'm probably the last person you want to see—"

I let out a *pfft* sound. My ribs sting with every word I say. "The last person I want to see left me bleeding in an alley."

I open my swollen eyes. Nori looks up, trying to balance the tears perched on her bottom lids. Her words are slow and quiet. "I knew he was angry, but I didn't think he would do this!"

The tears grow larger. She struggles to keep them on the edge. I sigh and grab her hand. She allows the tears to roll down her cheeks without a sound. I thought that would help her hold it in but girls are confusing.

She takes away her hand, wipes her face with her sleeves. After one final whimper, she stands resolute. "We have to do something about this."

Another knock on the door.

Expecting to see a doctor, the Nomad Village Police are standing in my room.

"Damon Doe. We'd like to get a statement from you, if you're feeling up to it. We were notified by the hospital that you are the victim of an assault by a minor."

Nori looks at me, her brown eyes unshakeable. She leans down and whispers to me. "This. Is. It." She turns to the two officers. "I'll wait in the lobby." She shuts the door so quick that her rose ponytail almost gets caught in the jamb.

🕐🕑🕒🕓🕔

Tuesday, December 5, 2017

I decided to tell the officers that Renner beat the snot out of me, but urged them not to press charges. I can't get answers if Renner is in a juvenile detention center. I did have the mind to explain why our altercation took place and that new evidence surfaced. I described the pocket watch and what we heard from the nosy neighbor. I also told them Renner's story and made sure to emphasize the book and his parents' disappearance. I know I don't have definitive proof that Renner's parents abducted us, but I think my desperate voice and pitiful physical state won the officers over. They said they would bring him in for questioning in the morning and that if I wanted to listen in, that they wouldn't stop me.

I'm discharged from the hospital with a few stitches on my forehead, severe facial and abdominal bruising, and a few broken ribs. Nori waits for me at the front. She hasn't left the hospital all night. The nurse who helped me in triage is still on call this morning so he rolls me to the door. I think seeing a young battered kid might have softened him up because he wished me luck and gave me a light pat on the back before leaving with the wheelchair.

Nori and I walk, laboring, to the police station. My legs are fine, but breathing proves difficult. She's quiet, chewing the inside of her cheek. I know she's disappointed I didn't press charges, but she said she understands my reasoning. The officers picked up Renner on his way to school and he is currently in the interrogation room. It's been four hours since he was brought in so I can't imagine he's in a good mood right now.

A tall, blond officer opens the door for us and says he's been waiting for us to arrive. A short, portly officer warns us that he's going in to question the teen and we better stay out of the observation room. He then winks at Nori and I and shuts the door behind him. The blond officer then nods toward the observation room door and walks back to his desk.

Nori leads the way since I'm so slow. She closes the door behind us and we watch the events unfold on a TV in the dark room. They must have a high-tech camera in there because the quality is crisp and the sound clear. Nori finds a chair and puts it behind me, holding my arm to lower my body gently into the seat. She stands behind me, her very presence emanating concern mixed with courage.

The portly officer sits across from Renner who looks exhausted and agitated. "Mr. Emit, I want you to know that although you could've faced a misdemeanor for juvenile assault, Damon is not going to press charges."

"My hero."

"Show some respect."

"Why? Everyone here is just going to take his side on everything so why bother with niceties?"

"Because, Mr. Emit, we brought you in to question you regarding the abductions of Damon and Nori. We haven't sided with anyone or you'd be in a cell instead of this room. Are you ready to cooperate?"

"Whatever."

The officer talks, but the audio cuts in and out like being on a phone call in the middle of a storm. I lean forward in my chair, hoping my proximity to the screen will change the state of the sound. Nori puts her hand on my shoulder and squeezes. The video is like a silent movie of Renner and the officer, without captions. I feel Nori's hand leave and I turn to see her halfway out the door, waving to the blond officer. He comes into the room and sighs.

"Sometimes this happens. The wireless connection between the camera and the feed is sometimes spotty. That's why we keep a secondary recording device on the table, for audio. This technology is supposed to make our lives easier, but it turns out to be more of a pain than anything else." He looks down at our destitute faces. "I'm sorry, guys. If it comes back on, great! If not, you'll have to wait until they are done to find out what he said."

Great. It feels like we're finally going to get some answers and we can't even hear them. The optimism growing in my chest dies a painful death. I don't know why I keep getting my hopes up. It's been a year and a half. I should just accept the fact that I'm not going to find out the truth and give up.

Suddenly on screen, Renner slams his hands on the table, stands up, points to the door, and exits the interrogation room. The portly officer stands up and joins the three of us in the observation room.

The blond officer asks what happened and the portly officer shrugs. "I questioned him about his childhood, how he ended up in the children's home. I asked him why the pocket watch found at the scene has his last name on it and he became enraged. He started mumbling under his breath about family and property. That's when he slammed his hands and yelled, asking me if he still needed to be here since he's not being charged. I had to say no and that's when he ran out. I'm sorry I couldn't do more guys."

"It's okay. Thank you both for everything you've done for us." Nori anchors her arm so I can pull myself out of the chair, feeling sorer than when I first sat down. I place my arm around her shoulders for a bit of support and shuffle to the front door.

"You have the watch with you, right Nori?"

We stop walking. She looks up at me and the color leaves her face. "No. Yesterday, I was rushing out of the house so fast to get to the hospital, I forgot to grab the watch."

"That's why he ran out. Renner's going to steal it."

"Oh shoot! It has my ring attached to the chain because I took it off to do the dishes for Miss Elle while she was gone. I didn't want to lose it down the drain."

Nori pops herself out from under my arm and runs back to the officers. She's waving her arms and pointing. The officers run out the door and pull their car up to the sidewalk. Nori opens the door and helps me get in. She runs around the other side and the portly officer grabs the door for her. The blond officer is driving and despite the amount of snow on the ground, he's doing well.

We get three quarters of the way to the children's home when we get stuck. The officer tried to take a back road, but instead got us stuck behind a village snowplow. The road is so narrow, we can't get around the giant, salt-throwing behemoth. Nori suggests we go on foot across the soybean field since it backs up to the children's home. The officers promise to meet us at the house as soon as they can get around the snowplow and we get out of the car. My abdomen burns from exerting so much effort. I'm going slow, but Nori doesn't say anything about it.

Any other day, I would've said the scene was beautiful. The sky is clear and for the first time in a month, we can see the sun. The snow on the field is thick and fluffy, shining in the sunlight. Today, it's a thorn in my bruised side. This snow and the state of my body are hindering me from Renner and it's infuriating. It takes ten minutes to cross the field before we reach the house. Nori runs ahead, through the back door. I get to the bottom of the porch stairs and stop to breath. The cold air cuts through my lungs. Nori returns to the porch.

"He's gone and so are the watch and my ring."

"I guess I'm not surprised. I bet, as soon as he found out the watch had his last name on it, he believed it was his. Your ring is just a consolation prize."

Miss Elle walks out, her face contorted with confusion. She squints in the unexpected sunlight. "Damon, what is going on? I just saw Renner run in and out of here and the police just pulled up out front."

"It's a long story. Let's get Damon inside and we'll explain what's going on."

Miss Elle watches Nori help me up the stairs like a child learning to walk. Miss Elle gets closer to me and clasps her hands to her mouth. She sobs and Nori embraces her. A moan escapes her hands. "Oh Damon."

I pat her shoulder from behind Nori. "It's okay. I'll be okay. Let's go inside."

Miss Elle looks at me again in horror and, with Nori, helps me inside the warm house.

🕐🕑🕒🕓🕔🕕

"**A**nd you are sure they were stolen?" The portly officer writes in his little notebook and stuffs it in his pocket.

"Yes. I left the ring attached to the watch in my shower caddy in the girl's bathroom. I've looked everywhere else to make sure I didn't leave them in a different place but..." Nori's voice trails into nothing. She looks up at me with her dark, wide eyes. I know she feels guilty for not bringing them with her, but she couldn't have known that Renner would take them.

"Maybe this is just a misunderstanding. Maybe Renner will come back and we can sit down and have an adult conversation about all of this." Miss Elle sniffles, fiddling with her knitting until she hears yelling from some littles in the living room. She puts her knitting on the dining table, stands up, and the freezes when her eyes on me again. They well up with heavy tears as she takes stock of my bruised and cut body. She glides over to me and places her arms carefully around my torso. I wrap my arms around her and squeeze until I can't bear the pain. I grab Miss Elle's shoulders and force her gaze to meet mine.

"I think you and I both know Renner is past the point of adult conversation."

Miss Elle takes my glasses off and wipes the almost invisible tears that were building at the corners of my swollen eyes. I've only been in the care of this woman for a year and a half, but she still knows exactly what to say and do to make me feel safe and loved. She hands me back my glasses, makes a loud sniffing noise, and heads into the living room with her body tight and stern, ready for discipline if necessary.

I put my glasses back on and lean against the dining room wall. I look to the blond officer, standing near the china cabinet across from me. "Can we press charges for petty theft?"

"Well, you could. I gotta be honest though, you would've been better off charging him for the assault."

"I don't want him in jail. I just want our stuff back."

The portly officer speaks up, "Didn't you say the watch has his last name on it and was taken from his former home?"

I look at Nori. She hangs her head low and confirms the officer's statement.

"Do you have any evidence that proves the ring is yours, Nori?"

She shakes her head again, biting the inside of her lip.

"Then you can't press charges for theft. There's more evidence against the two of you than him at this point." The officer studies Nori's somber face and his demeanor loosens. "Look, I know you want answers for your amnesia and I'm sorry we can't give them to you. If you really think Renner and his family had something to do with your possible abductions, then you need to find him."

"We could file a missing person's report." Nori pops up from the table, her voice higher than usual.

The portly officer glances at the blond officer and they nod. "We'll go back to the station and file the report. We have enough information from his earlier questioning. We'll call you if we need more."

The two men walk to the dining room door when Nori stops them. "Wait!" The men pause. "You've been so kind to us throughout all of this. Most of the time adults don't listen to teenagers, especially when they have bizarre stories of amnesia and abduction. Before you go, what are your names?"

The portly officer smiles. "I'm Officer Burg and this is Officer Ergo."

"Thank you for your help."

The men nod and leave Nori and I alone in the dining room. Nori turns to me. "Do you think we'll find him?"

"I'm not sure."

"Maybe you should check in your room to see if he grabbed anything of yours." She pushes in her chair, walks over, and places herself under my arm for support while we walk to the boy's room. She stops in front of the door, no girls allowed.

The other boys are still at school so I'm alone, moving sloth-like, using the other bed frames to keep me upright. When I get to the back, our bunk looks the same as it did before school yesterday. Beds unkempt. Clothes in piles. Books stacked.

Books!

I stick my arm under Renner's pillow and my belly fills with hope again. The only thing I haven't checked for clues, the one thing that might bring Renner out of hiding is in my grasp.

Walden.

🕐🕑🕒🕓🕔

"I learned this, at least, by my experiment: that if one advances confidently in the direction of his dreams, and endeavors to live the life which he has imagined, he will meet with a success unexpected in common hours." I shut the book and pull the ice pack away from my face. Some of the swelling is down after a two-hour nap and medicine. Searching through this book makes me want to take another nap. Drool leaks from the corner of Nori's mouth as she snuggles in the giant afghan Miss Elle just made. I know she took Renner's side at first but with everything that has happened over the past day, I'm not sure what I would do without her. She's kind, smart, and beautiful. She considers others before herself and has a natural ability with children. I know it's been a short time together, but I'm starting to think she could be my—

Nori makes a loud, surprising noise and rockets out of the chair. Her eyes fix on me and widen, her hands shoot up to her face to cover it. A bemoaned *ohhhh* sound follows as she shrinks back into the chair. She pulls the blanket over her head like a tent and sighs.

It's difficult not to laugh at the dramatics, but I keep my composure. "You okay?"

Another sigh escapes the holes of the blanket. "Yep. Just an embarrassing dream."

"Oh, now you have to tell me what that was about!"

"Nope! Thanks for the offer though!"

I walk over and snatch the blanket from her head. Her fiery hair sticks out in every direction, the sound of static electricity crackling in the air. She tries to tame it, but it's too late. "Nope, nope, nope. Definitely nope."

I toss the blanket back at her and she resumes her burrowed position. "Come on. At least with the blanket over your head, you can see my face through the holes, but I can't see yours."

Silence fills the room. I imagine her yarn-draped, internal struggle. Just when I think she's going to decline me once more, the blanket moves. "It was about our wedding day."

I burst into laughter. Nori shoots out of the blanket and hits me with it. "Stop it!" Her hair electrified once again makes me gasp for air between howls.

"Damon! This is so embarrassing!"

"Was I ruggedly handsome?"

"Of course, you want to know what *you* looked like in the dream." She sits down on the couch next to me and tosses her hair into a bun. I'm astonished how girls can do that so fast. Or how they can wrap their hair up in a towel.

"We were adults. We still looked like ourselves, just more mature. You had facial hair and your body grew, well, it grew."

"Nice! Lanky nerd for the win!"

"I know I said the dream was embarrassing, but more than that."

"Yes?"

"It felt real."

"Well, you were with me so—"

"Shut up!" She whacks me with the blanket again. "The smell of fresh lilies, the fabric of my dress. All of it. It was like I was remembering it, not just dreaming." Her eyes draw me in. A tingle travels down my spine. I swallow hard and lean in. She pulls toward me and closes her eyes.

"You guys find anything in Renner's—Oh!" Miss Elle bursts through the door. Nori and I jump from the surprise and smack foreheads. "Um, uh, I'll go make you a snack!" Miss Elle says a little too loud and darts into the kitchen, letting the door swing closed behind her. Nori and I rub our foreheads and force fake laughs.

Nori looks at me, but diverts her eyes to the kitchen door. "I'll go help her!"

I'm left alone with *Walden* in my lap and the giant afghan lying next to me. I pick up the blanket to put over my head, but think better of getting into a shame spiral right now. I clutch the book and head into the kitchen.

🕐🕑🕒🕓🕔

"In the front cover of the book, there's a dedication: *Happy Birthday, Renner! We hope this book inspires you as much as it inspires us. Love, your Dad and Mom*. The rest contains Henry David Thoreau's thoughts on nature and independence and little handwritten inscriptions every few pages. The handwriting is different from the initial dedication and they say things like *I love you more than the stars in the sky* and *your parents will come back for you soon.* The book is falling apart. It's in such bad shape, the dust cover is stuck to the last page of the book. There's nothing helpful in here."

Nori takes a bite of her apple, still looking a little frazzled from our close encounter in the living room. Miss Elle paces the kitchen, probably wishing she had announced herself before walking into the couch room earlier.

"You need to find him, Damon."

I almost choke on my lemonade. "Not happening."

"Miss Elle has a point. We have no other leads. Renner is missing. Maybe we should go—"

"Let me get right on that." I pick up my cup and sip.

A wrinkled finger enters my view. "That was not a request! You *must* go find Renner. I know you believe he and his family are the keys to your conundrum, so go find him! Get to the bottom of this once and for all!" Miss Elle snatches the cup from my hands. "Let me know if you need me to take you somewhere." She leaves, probably to prepare for the middles and teens getting home from school.

"Where do we go first?"

"First the archery field. Then maybe school. After that, I'm out of ideas."

"It's a start."

🕐🕑🕒🕓🕔

We searched the archery field, but it was blanketed in fresh snow. There wasn't a single footprint for a mile.

No one saw Renner at school this afternoon, but knowing him, he wouldn't hide out there. The police are keeping an eye out for him and the school has cameras outside and in the halls. They said they'd called the children's home if they saw him.

Nori and I sit in a booth at the pizza place, waiting for our food. Miss Elle's snack, while generous, didn't quite cut it for Nori. She digs into her pizza the moment the waitress puts it on the table. No pretenses or giant blankets to hide under, Nori is elbow deep in mozzarella. My stomach turns. It was exactly 24 hours ago that I had the daylights knocked out of me in alley just outside. I haven't eaten since going to the hospital, but I just can't bring myself to eat. My insides growl and sour simultaneously.

After Nori stuffs her face with the entire pizza, she looks puzzled. "What if Renner went to the abandoned house?"

"Why would he go there?"

"It was his childhood home. He knows the address."

"It's probably a trap. He wants us to go there so he and his family can abduct us again and do who-knows-what."

Nori slides out of the booth and extends her hand out to me. "I've got an idea."

I scoot down the booth, my sides screaming in pain. I reach out to take her hand, and just before we touch, a tiny electric spark jumps from my hand to hers, shocking us. We pull our hands away and rub the tips of our fingers. Nori smiles at me and extends her hand a second time. I return the smile, my heart pounding, and take her hand to leave.

XI

The house seems peaceful. The evening sky darkens with drifting clouds. With the high winds, a layer of fresh snow covers the graffiti on the siding. The yard is untouched and sparkling. A set of footprints leads to the door and the police tape is missing.

It's time to learn the truth, once and for all.

I breathe a sigh and the air vapors in front of me. I reach down to grab Nori's hand. She locks her fingers in mine and holds tight, her right-hand clutching Thoreau's brittle dust cover. I lead the way down the sidewalk to the porch.

The door is cracked open.

I look down at Nori and give her tiny hand a squeeze. She squeezes back and looks up at me from beneath her plaid scarf. Two braids contain her glowing hair beneath a knit beanie with a fuzz ball on top.

I hesitate as I push the door. The temperature causes the hinges to creak with agony. If he didn't know we were here, he does now. Might as well announce ourselves. I open my mouth to speak, but am interrupted by a soft voice.

"Renner. It's Nori. I—I'm here with Damon. We just want to talk."

Out of the two of us, she's the brave one.

She's as strong as iron.

I take a step forward into the living room and something shatters beneath my shoe. I pick up my foot and realize I've stepped on the same pottery I broke a year and a half ago. I sweep the ceramic pieces to the side and pull my whole body and Nori's inside.

Nori's hand trembles for a second. I wouldn't have noticed if I hadn't been so aware of her hand in mine. Going inside won't affect me since I try to separate myself from that incident as much as possible. But for Nori, it's only been a few months and I'm beginning to think this was a stupid plan.

Nori releases my hand and reaches into her back pocket. Out of my periphery, a small light turns from red to green. Nori returns her hand to mine, which unfortunately for her, got a bit sweaty. We take a few more steps onto the living room carpet and hear creaking in the dark opening ahead of us.

It's my turn to be brave.

"Renner, please, let's figure this out together."

A cough comes from the shadows. "It's a little late for that, don't you think?" He opens the watch face and the purple light glows in the darkness. His face glows sinister as he rubs his thumb on the glass surface. Nori's ring pulses purple on the chain of the watch. He looks up at me, his dark eyes cloud with rage. "Why didn't you tell me about this?"

"We were going to!" Nori's voice is dry, like the words are stuck in her throat.

"We were?" I turn toward her and let go of her hand. Her eyes widen with panic, as if I ruined her original plan. "I was not going to tell you about the watch and the ring, well, that isn't even yours."

Renner steps into the light rays the front door is casting onto the floor. He shuts the watch cover and dangles the timepiece by the chain. "If Nori had looked inside the ring at the inscription, she'd see it says Emit too."

Nori's breath catches.

Renner's voice rumbles. "What do you want from me?"

"Tell us the truth. What happened to us? Where are your parents? Why would you come back here if you didn't know anything?"

Renner swings the pocket watch back and forth. "This watch and ring mean more to you than my friendship. After everything I've done for you, especially you Damon. This is how you repay me? You steal items from this house that do not belong to you? They have *my* name on them!"

"I'll admit, I grabbed the watch before I was found by the police, but when I first woke up, the ring was already on my finger." Nori tries to step toward Renner, but he holds up his palm to halt her.

"I came back here because I knew you'd try to find me. And I promised myself when you did, I would destroy the things you care about most, just like you did to me." He pulls on the watch chain and the timepiece flies in the air. He catches it and my heart drops into my stomach.

"Renner, please, don't do that."

Why did I say that?

"I'm not a monster, you know. My family is not who you think they are."

Nori finds her voice again. "You are a victim of circumstance. Your parents left you with your grandmother when you were just a baby and then she died because of this tragic fire." Renner peaks over his left shoulder toward the wreckage. "It's not your fault you ended up in the children's home, Renner."

"No, but it's Damon's fault I've lost everything else."

My stomach is a ball of emotions. I'm angry he's blaming me. I'm sad our friendship is over. I'm worried he's might do something to the watch and the ring.

"You haven't lost everything, Renner. You even forgot something." I point to Nori and she holds up *Walden* for Renner to see.

His eyes grow large and he shouts. "Give me the book!"

Nori and I flinch. "Give us the watch and ring first."

"Yeah right. I know what these mean to you. You'll find some way to use them against me. You'll get the police to investigate them to prove that my family had something to do with your possible abduction and amnesia problem. Nice try." He continues tossing the watch and letting it fall closer to the ground before scooping it up at the last second. Every time he does, my heart jumps.

I look down at Nori and her eyes plead.

"Do it."

Her eyes well up with tears.

"Start from the back." This is our last hope.

She opens the back cover of the book and grabs the page stuck to the dust cover and rips. The sound echoes through the room, followed by shout from Renner.

"Stop!"

"Renner, hand over the watch and ring or Nori will keep ripping."

Tears roll down Nori's face as she holds the freshly torn page. She told me she didn't want to do this, but I talked her into it.

"That book connects me to my family." He's still shouting, causing more tears to flow from Nori's eyes.

Anger overtakes me. "Our memories are lost. We have no family. Nowhere to go. We don't even know our *real* names! I'll destroy the book myself if it means you'll finally tell us what happened."

Renner's eyes change from cloudy brown rage to light hazel

sorrow and turns to Nori. "Please Nori! Look at what you are doing! You don't want to do this." His voice grows frantic. "My grandmother's writing is in there. Look at it!"

Nori looks at the page in her hand. She furrows her brow and brings the page closer to her face. Dropping the book, she falls to her knees.

"Nori!"

Nori's left hand holds her mouth while the right shakes with the page.

"Don't move, Damon, or I'll shatter them." He swings the watch like a pendulum.

She covers her eyes and rubs her forehead.

My heart is racing.

What's happening to her?

"Please, Renner, she could be hurt."

"I SAID DON'T MOVE!"

She rocks back and forth on the ground and I'm frozen in place. Nausea hits my stomach and I almost double over seeing her in this state.

"Renner, please!"

"SHUT UP!"

Nori gasps as if she had been drowning, but can breathe again. The sound silences Renner and I both. She stops rocking and rises with care. She turns to me and her complexion matches the snow outside. Tears roll down her cheeks.

"I remember."

"What?"

"Look at this." Nori hands me the torn piece of paper. The front is blank but the back, which was stuck to the book, is covered in handwritten letters and symbols. My vision flickers like a strobe, but this time it's different. It comes at me like a flood breaking loose from a dam.

⏰⏰⏰⏰⏰

Tuesday, September 5, 2000

B alloons. Streamers. Cake. A banner on the wall that reads, "Happy 1st Birthday!"

"Sweetheart, do you know where we put our present for the baby?" I call from the dining room as I rummage through the china hutch. I take notice in the display windows that I skipped a hole on my dress shirt. My large hands fumble with the delicate buttons, my wedding ring shimmers in the reflection. I take stock of the man before me. I stand tall with a shadow descending over my jaw and chin. My hair is dark with hints of age, styled wavy to the right of my part. Dust clouds my reflection, but focus my eyes on the small particles covering back of my glasses. I replace my cleaned lenses to my nose and smile, my blue eyes still keen with youth.

Nori walks in the dining room, laughing at my moment of arrogance. Her laced-up wedges echo as she moves across the hardwood floors. She reaches out a hand to assist me in fixing my shirt. I forgot I wasn't done with that yet. She tucks a stray hair into her neat, red bun, the streaks of white glistening in the light of the fall afternoon sun.

"To answer your question, I'm not sure we is the word you are looking for since you put it in the attic a few weeks ago." She chuckles, spins around so her plaid dress whips the side of my leg, and clicks back into the kitchen to finish the birthday meal.

Her floral scent draws me to the kitchen door and I poke my head around the corner. Stirring a boiling pot of noodles, she starts the microwave. Nori walks to the kitchen table where our sweet baby watches from his highchair. She bends down so she is eye to eye with the boy. His dark, inquisitive eyes stare into her soul. Nori wiggles a finger under his double chin and the boy squeals with laughter.

"It's your birthday today, isn't it? How old are you my sweet boy?"

The baby throws his arms in the air with purpose and makes an unintelligible declaration. Nori gives a bright toothy smile.

"That's right, my son! You are one-year-old today!" She tickles one of his fat feet and glides back to the stove. "I thought you were getting the present from the attic."

I stand up straight, eyes wide, like a kid caught with his hand in a cookie jar. "I, uh, forgot something in the kitchen!"

"Really?" She throws a hand on her hip and narrows her eyes. Her sass is extra sassy today. I like it.

I stride toward my wife, wrap an arm around the small of her back, and dip her into a kiss. When I pull away, Nori's hazel eyes look dazed from the unexpected smooch. She blinks a few times; I imagine it's to help her return to reality. We smile and I take my leave.

I make my way down the hall and pull the string to the attic stairs. I'm careful in my movements because the picture frames on the wall only leave a small margin of room to unwrap the stairs. The hall is lined with photographs and awards. There are the childhood photos of Nori and I next to pictures of our graduations, both high school and college. I call this the "wall of shame." I don't miss being short or lanky. Nori looks the same, in the best way possible. The wall's one redeeming quality is our display of college degrees. A Bachelor of Arts in Psychology and a Master of Arts in Marriage and Family Counseling awarded to Nori Selah Pilut and a Doctorate of Science in Biochemistry conferred to Dr. Marc Damon Emit. For me, it was the only degree worth displaying since it was the most challenging of them all.

On the opposite wall, our wedding memories artistically arranged with a frame for the invitation and program. The most elaborate of all is the collage of the baby's monthly snapshots, comparing how the little chunk has grown over the past eleven months. I move the ladder with caution, avoiding the memories lining my walls.

The ladder is rickety, the attic humid. I duck my head and pull the chain to click on the light. Peering around the shadows, I try to recall where I put my son's present. I hear a yell from the kitchen.

"Honey, why did you hide it in the attic in the first place? Anywhere taller than our son would've been perfectly fine."

I laugh, "I want to get used to hiding things up here because our son is a genius and will easily find our regular hiding spots in the future." I turn around and see our boxes of Christmas ornaments and remember that I put the gift in the box labeled "tree." Reaching through the artificial branches, I feel the small wrapped present. I pull it out, return the lid, and click the light off.

As soon as the light dissipates, something catches my eye. A purple glow emanates at the edge of the attic floor. I lay the present on the top stair and step across the joists toward the violet light. I crouch down, lean against the rafter to keep my balance, and reach. As soon as I pick it up, I realize it's a pocket watch, but before I can get a good look at it, the purple glow brightens to an intense fluorescence and in an instant, dissolves into the darkness. I crawl out of attic; still a bit blinded from the purple light with present in one hand, watch in the other.

The doorbell chimes. "Nori, will you get that? I'm trying not to destroy memories with this ladder."

"I'm elbow deep in a baby diaper right now so you are going to have to get it!"

I close the hatch, avoiding any framed casualties, and jog through the living room to open the front door. A short woman with silver hair and a flowing purple dress stands at the door. I look down at the guest and smile.

"Hey, Mom!" I hug her stout figure and usher her into the house. Nori turns the corner, a fresh baby on her hip. "Ailia! Welcome!"

"You better hand the birthday boy over to his Oma right now! She has traveled too far to wait!" The child leans over to his grandmother who catches him and spins him around. After they finish spinning, the boy bursts into laughter as my mom showers him in sloppy, loud kisses. She stops turns to me. "Let me get a good look at you, son."

I sigh, "Mother, I'm thirty-two, married, with a son and a doctorate. I'm hardly a boy!"

My mom laughs as she takes stock of me. Locking eyes with my hands, she interjects with fear in her voice. "Where did you get that?"

I look down. "Oh, I got it at the bookstore. It's one of my favorite classic memoirs on life and nature. I know the baby is too young to read it but—"

"Not the book, the watch!" She grabs my wrist to turn my hand in display.

"That? It was glowing purple in the attic and I grabbed it just before you got here. I'm not even sure where it came from." Nori locks eyes with me with question in her gaze. I turn to my mother, who lost all color from her face.

Mother hands the baby back to Nori, panting as if out of breath. "We need to discuss something regarding that pocket watch." She walks over to the chair near the window and sits down. I follow while Nori puts our son in the jumperoo next to the couch.

"Damon. I know you don't want me to bring it up, but under the circumstances, I have no choice." She swallows hard as she fiddles with her fingers. "That watch belonged to your father."

"What?" I furrow my brow, scratching my neck with one hand while putting the timepiece down on the coffee table in front of me with the other. "You're right. I don't want you to bring it up."

Nori takes hold of my clenched hand. "Keep going, Ailia. It's better if everything is out in the open."

"I understand your animosity toward your father, but Nolon was a good man—"

"A good man abandons his family?" I roar as I jump up from the couch and start pacing. My sudden change in volume and position causes the baby to cry.

Mother waves for me to sit back down as Nori cuddles our son.

"Listen. That watch belonged to your father, and his father and his father's father. It has been in the possession of the first-born male of the Emit family for three generations."

"Why does that matter?"

My mom's gaze locks with mine. "It matters because your father didn't abandon us. He was a time traveler."

I burst into laughter. "Is this because of the research I've started at the university? Did President Gereg put you up to this? Where are the hidden cameras?"

My mom shakes her head and watches her now sleeping grandbaby as Nori lays him into the bassinet. "I know it is hard to believe, but your father, his father, and your great-grandfather, traveled back in time to protect history. In Berlin, your great-grandfather Otto bought that pocket watch at a small trinket shop. When he got home, it was revealed to him the capabilities of the watch, time travel. He grew scared of the power this timepiece offered and went back to the trinket shop to return it. When he reached the street, the shop was no longer there."

Nori looks up and my mom's hands. "Ailia. How is this possible?"

"You believe her?" I snap.

Nori jerks her head toward me. "I'm trying to understand."

My mom stands up, picks up the watch, and hands it to me. "Look at it, Damon. Your great-grandfather Otto found our family name inscribed on the back trying to return the watch."

I flip the watch to the back and Emit shines in the light. "Mother, that doesn't prove anything."

She takes the watch from my hand, clicks a few of the buttons on the side, and a sliver of paper pops out from a nearly invisible seam. The paper is about an inch wide and an inch long. The paper lengthens as she pulls until it is out as far is it will go. She reads the written message:

The house of Emit now conceals a paradox, which pertains to the treatment of clocks. Backwards through time one can travel, to protect generations from evil unravel. Beware; when one revolves time forward, the years will retreat physically rearward. Heed the warning of advancing your turn that someday one's life must again be relearned.

My mom gives the paper a quick tug and it retracts back into the watch, concealing it.

I decide to play along. "So, you are telling me that the reason Dad was barely visible in our lives is because he was a time traveler?"

"Yes. Nolon's grandfather Otto fed those who were starving in America during the Great Depression. His father Siris helped Jews escape from the Łódź ghetto in Poland during World War II. Your father traveled to Brazil in the 1970's to help the dissidents starving in their tenets while they fought against military dictatorship. They went back in time to help those who were helpless, Damon. Your father is a hero of time."

"I need some air." I know I was playing around before, but the conviction in my mother's voice is too much to bear. I shuffle through the living room and out the back door. I stare off the porch, toward a sunset of purple and pink.

"She's telling the truth." Nori scoots up next to me on the railing. "I think you know that deep down, don't you?"

I take in a deep breath and look at my wife. "I have an insatiable interest in how the world works, especially on a scientific level. I've devoted my entire career to researching the complexities of life. Logic and reason aside, I know my mother is telling the truth." I take off my glasses to rub my eyes. "You know as well as anyone, I've always been fascinated by time. Growing up, my friends thought it was weird that instead of talking about ninjas and warriors, I wanted to discuss time space continuums or time travel. Come to find out, my father, grandfather, and great-grandfather lived out the one thing I want to know most about."

As I put my glasses back on, I hear the sliding door open. My mother, holding my sleeping son, steps out and sits on the porch swing. "I'm sorry I never told you, Damon. Your father was very protective of this family secret. You see this pocket watch has another secret message." She holds the silver timepiece and clicks a button three times. Another inch of paper pops out of the side. "This message is a prophecy specific to the Emit family. Your great-grandfather Otto warned his son Siris of the message. Siris foretold it to your father, and Nolon, well, he thought it was about you." She hands the watch to me. I pull the paper as far is it will go and read:

> The firstborn son, the fifth generation of Emit, will betray his family, by destroying the power within it. If he willfully damages the watch in his midst, the bloodline of Emit will cease to exist.

My mother keeps her voice quiet as she swings the baby. "That's why your father was so distant. He gone for years, helping others in time, but he tried to protect you from the possibility of this prophecy at the same time. If this watch and the power it offers is destroyed, it would be catastrophic. The timeline would reset. All the good done by your father and those before him would be erased. The timeline would be forever changed and even worse, our linage would erase from existence. Your father didn't want to put that kind of pressure on you so he hid the watch and made me promise to never tell you about it."

I speed read the prophecy to myself and tug so it returns to its secret compartment.

"But Mom, the prophecy isn't about me. The fifth generation of Emit is my son." I freeze and stare at my precious sleeping child.

"The prophecy is about Renner."

XII

I feel like I could puke from the head rush I just experienced. I blink a few times to make sure I'm back in the present. I look on a teenage Nori and tears stream down her face. I reach out and she lays a hand into mine. "Oh honey."

"Wait." She yanks on something beneath her jacket. A cord hangs limp in her grasp as she pulls the battery pack from her back pocket. She switches the light back to red and chucks it out into the snow.

"Honey?"

His voice jars me. I almost forgot Renner was standing there. I don't even want to look at him.

I'm so ashamed.

"You couldn't have known, sweetheart." Nori reaches, cups my cheek, and strokes it with her delicate thumb.

"Sweetheart?"

His voice shreds my insides. Tears break loose from my lids. Nori wipes them away. "But, how did you get here?"

"WILL SOMEONE PLEASE TELL ME WHAT IS GOING ON?"

Jolted again, I turn to face my son. It's the first time I see him as my son. I sigh and tears fall down my face again. Nori squeezes my hand.

"Renner, we need to tell you something."

"What did you throw outside?"

"A wire. I was wearing it to record your confession, but that's not what's important anymore."

"I can't believe this." Renner begins pacing. "You still think I know what happened to you guys? I don't!"

I clear my throat, "We know."

He jerks his head up and stares at me. He has his mother's eyes and my unruly hair. *I can't believe how grown he is.* I find the words I need. "I know you aren't going to believe this, but we're your parents."

Renner makes a sour face. "That's ridiculous. Is this a joke?"

"You said your father and mother abandoned you when you were a child and left you with your grandmother."

"I've told you that before, Damon. You already knew that."

"Your father used the watch in your hand to travel forward in time."

At this moment, I remember I left Nori behind. "You didn't tell me how you got here."

"I used the ring. Your mother used that ring to check on your father when he would travel back in time. Your great-grand-mother bought it from the same shop your great-grandfather purchased the watch, but neither of them knew they were connected until he learned how to use the watch. If I spin the ring on my finger three times clockwise, it'll take me to whenever you are in time. If I spin it three times counterclockwise, it'll take me back to when I first left."

"Why did you come?"

"A whole year went by and you didn't return. Ailia worried too so she gave me the ring, taught me how to use it, and then I left. It was four in the afternoon when I left." She turns to Renner. "We didn't understand the repercussions of traveling forward in time."

Renner paces faster, staring at the watch and the ring. "This can't be real. It just can't!"

Nori continues, "We lost our memories and our identities. When the police tried to fingerprint us, it smudged. That was a consequence of traveling forward in time, well that and the amnesia. The watch warned what would happen if we went forward instead of backward, but the message was cryptic."

"Here, let me show you the messages, Renner—"

I try to take a step forward but Renner shouts, "Don't come any closer!" His eyes are frantic and confused.

"Renner." He stops at the sound of Nori's voice. "If you won't let us show you, take this." She holds up the page she ripped from the book. She takes a small step forward and then another. Her arm stretches forward and Renner snatches the paper.

He stares at it and then looks at the watch. He pushes a few buttons and the first piece of paper pops out. He reads to himself. He pushes another button three times and reads the warning of the fifth Emit son. I see him mouthing the words, but no sounds escape.

"You guys did this to a random watch. You found a watch in a pawn shop and put these messages in it to prank me. This isn't real."

"It's real, Renner. I'm your father."

His voice grows loud again, "My father's name was—"

"Marc Damon Emit."

Renner paces again. "I've never told you that! You probably found it online somewhere!"

"Didn't you think it was strange that out of all the names in the whole world, I chose your father's middle name? I remember the look on your face when I introduced myself to you. Or how you reacted when you heard Nori chose your mother's first name, Nori Selah? Renner, we both *appeared* in your childhood home on your birthday."

"Coincidences exist. Things happen randomly all the time."

"While that may be true, your father left from this living room on your first birthday, and I left on your second birthday, to come to the present to stop you from what you are doing now."

I shake my head in shame. "I'm afraid our time travel solution is the cause of the problem in the first place."

Renner's pacing speeds up, his hands clench in fists. "Do you really expect me to believe this? You two should be committed! You're both teenagers!"

It's all dawning on me. "The first message of the pocket watch states that if we travel forward, we age backward. We traveled through time at the same rate as the present. We thought it would be instantaneous. I set the watch forward fifteen years, but that's how long it took me to get here. Nori, that ring followed the same time constraints as the watch. When we arrived in the future, we lost our memories and had to relearn them. The page your grandmother wrote in the back of this book sparked our memories, Renner."

Nori puts her arm around my waist. I missed her touch without even knowing it was gone. "Damon, your mom told me to take that paper with me because it explained how the watch and ring worked but it was too late, I was already spinning the ring. She must've glued the instructions to the back of *Walden* and hoped Renner would still have the book when we finally got here."

My mother.

Tears fall down my cheeks again.

My mother is dead because of me.

My son grew up without a family, in a children's home, because of me.

I've ruined everything.

Renner stops pacing. "Prove it. Prove you are my parents and I'll believe you."

Nori speaks with a calm tone. "Go down the hall and stop just before you get to the attic hatch. There are baby pictures of you on the walls. Your father and I both have our degrees hanging up. There's even a picture of your Grandma Ailia."

Renner disappears into the darkness of the hall. I can't bear to follow him. I hear him stop, the purple glow of the watch bounces off the walls. A squeaking sound, probably removing the soot from the glass, is followed by a sudden crash. Shattering. He walks out to the living room and tosses our first family photo on the floor in front of us.

He stares. Standing in this broken, wasted home, his dark eyes pierce my soul. He takes a deep breath and runs his hands over his face. Anger and shock are fighting as fire ignites in his gaze. He zips his coat as high as it will go. His jaw clenches, fists squeeze, but paces again. He lets out a groan like the sound a bear makes when it is wounded but decides to continue protecting itself despite its obvious injury.

He stops. His knees buckle. Dropping to the dusty carpet, his eyes show something new, hurt. He unzips his jacket and slams it to the ground. He holds a hand to his mouth and rocks back and forth, fighting shouts and tears. I stand paralyzed at the fall of my child.

"How could you?"

"We thought we were doing the right thing. The prophecy stated the fifth generation and that was you. Your father thought it smart to travel forward to stop you, but we didn't know this would be the outcome."

"YOU. ABANDONED. ME."

I sniffle.

"You left me. You left me and never gave me a chance."

I'm so disappointed in myself.

"Why didn't you trust that I would do the right thing? Why did you let some old cryptic watch decide that I would destroy our family without even giving me a chance to prove it wrong?"

I'm so ashamed.

"I need some air." Renner walks toward us, I brace myself for impact, but he slides passed the two of us to go out the front door.

Nori embraces me and we sob. After a minute, she pulls away from me. "We should go check on him."

We walk outside. Renner is gone. He still has the watch and the ring.

🕐🕑🕒🕓🕔

The police drive us back to the children's home. We know Renner won't be there, but we want to say goodbye. Walking up the sidewalk to the place I've called home for a year and a half is surreal. Nori wipes away snow from the front sign. She's gentle as she cleans the slush off each letter.

"My great-grandmother started this home. She was an orphan and wanted children like her to have a warm place to sleep while they waited for their forever home. Who knew it would also keep our son warm someday?" Her eyes well up.

"Let me do the talking." She takes my hand and nods.

I open the door. The air is warm and smells like biscuits and gravy. Breakfast for dinner, my favorite. I lead Nori to the kitchen and Viv is in there helping Miss Elle wash the dishes.

"Damon! Nori! Hey!" She drops down from the step stool, arms covered in soap suds and water, and tackles me with a hug. I squeeze her tight. She leans over and wraps her arms around Nori's neck. Nori sniffles, fighting a sob.

"Hey Viv, we need to talk to Miss Elle. Can you make sure all the littles have brushed their teeth and are tucked in for bed?"

She salutes me like she would a lieutenant and marches out of the kitchen. I'm going to miss that girl.

"Well, did you find him?" Miss Elle scrubs a baking pan and drops it into the soapy water. After searching Nori's face, her own shifts to worry.

I clear my throat. "We have to leave, Miss Elle."

Miss Elle pauses. "I knew this day would come."

Huh?

"Fourteen years ago, I got a phone call from a good friend from my knitting circle. She told me she was in the hospital and wasn't doing well. Remembering that I ran the children's home, she made me promise that if something happened to her that I would keep an eye on her beautiful, brown-eyed grandson. My friend also mentioned that his parents might come back for him around Renner's birthday, September 5th. Ailia said it wouldn't be in a conventional way, but told me not to get involved, even if things seemed weird."

I'm speechless.

"She told me your full names and described what you looked like. She didn't know you would be teenagers again, but thought any details might help."

Wow.

"I've been on this earth a long time and I've seen a lot of crazy...stuff. Time travel isn't outside of my realm of belief."

Nori lunges for Miss Elle and hugs her tight. She whispers into her ear.

"You're welcome." Miss Elle looks up at me, eyes wet with tears. "I would do it all over again if I had to." She reaches her hand out to me. I take it into mine, lean forward, and give her a kiss on the cheek. "But don't make me. Go get your son."

I peel Nori off Miss Elle and say one last goodbye to the

woman who has cared so much for my family and me. We meander out the door and seal it behind us. Our situation is too hard to explain to the others in the home and I don't think I would have the willpower to leave if I had to face them again.

🕐🕑🕒🕓🕔

We move at a snail's pace up the path so we don't startle him. Snow covers the ground, lone footprints lead straight to him and his target. Lights tied to various trees illuminate the field. Clouds mask the stars, threatening snow. The pocket watch and ring are pinned to the target so the timepiece hangs centered in bullseye.

He searches through his quiver and plucks out an arrow. He fits it to the string and pulls back. The arrow cuts through the silence and my stomach drops when it lands just below the watch. I've seen him shoot before. That was on purpose.

"Son—"

"No."

"We're so sorry."

He lets us get about a foot away before he lets another arrow fly, this time hitting just to the right of our lifeline.

Nori advances without fear and puts her hand on his shoulder. "Renner. We did what we thought was right, but we were wrong."

Renner drops his shoulder so her hand falls off. She steps back in line and leans into me.

My turn.

"I should've trusted that when you were old enough, you would make the right decision. That despite what the prophecy said, you wouldn't betray our family."

He releases another arrow, striking to the left, boxing-in the watch.

"So where does that leave us?"

Nori speaks from behind me, "It's up to you now. You can release that final arrow, destroying the watch and erasing our family from time, you included. You can give us the pocket watch and we can go back to your 1st birthday to fix this. Or you can keep the watch and the ring and your father and I will continue to live our lives from this point forward, knowing we can never take it back."

A chuckle forces its way from Renner's lips. "I'm obviously not going to destroy it."

I stare into his eyes. "How do you want time to unfold, Renner?"

He walks to the target and unpins it. Holding the ring in one hand and the watch in the other, the engraved *Emit* shines in the lights. Snowflakes fall around us, settling like the calm following the shake of a snow globe.

Epilogue

Sunday, September 5, 2010

A quiet knock echoes through the home. The glider slows to a halt. She rises, careful not to wake the sleeping baby in her arms. Floating to the door, she admires the child's curly, golden hair. The baby yawns and stretches as best she can in her tight swaddle. Her emerald eyes gaze sleepily on the timeworn woman smiling down on her.

The elder opens the door and a couple waits patiently, expectantly. She puts a wrinkled finger to her lips and points down at the again sleeping bundle. The early middle-aged couple follows her into the living room and sits on a couch next to the glider. They admire the newborn from afar, their hearts anxious with love. The caretaker reaches out with the baby and lays her into the arms of the man. She squirms for a second, but settles with a smile in the corner of her mouth. His crystal blue eyes well up as he absorbs the child's warmth, glasses streaked from his tear-soaked lashes. Rubbing the baby's curls between her fingers, the woman's breath catches in her chest.

Enthralled with the gift they've received, they do not notice the senior stepping out of the room. She returns with a pink bag, filled with the baby's possessions. The couple rises from the couch and the wife accepts the bag. The husband places the newborn back into the arms of the elder for one last goodbye. The baby frees a hand from her swaddle and reaches for the salt and pepper waves sitting on the elder's shoulders. The woman gives the child a gentle kiss on the forehead and hands her back to her new father.

The couple gets the baby strapped into the car before waving to the caretaker. She blows a kiss into the air for the newborn and her new family.

⊙⊙⊙⊙⊙

T he couple arrives home. The husband's mother greets them at the door with a shining smile. "I'll go get him." The grandmother disappears from the room as the couple removes the baby from the car seat and swaddles her in a bright, soft blanket.

A boy enters the room and stops in the doorway. His dark eyes look on the child with fear and anticipation, hugging a thick book to his chest. Eleven years on this earth as an only child and today changes everything. He scratches his brown mop of hair as he waits for his parents to notice him.

His mother looks up from the baby in her arms and beams at her firstborn son. She tucks a fiery strand of hair behind her ear. "Renner, come meet your new baby sister, Viv."

Appendix of Names

In case you missed it, all* fictional names in this book are palindromes or semordnilaps.

Palindrome = A word that reads the same forwards and backwards

Semordnilap = A word that forms a different word when written in reverse.

I've categorized them below for your viewing pleasure:

Palindrome Names	Semordnilap Names
Renner	Damon (Nomad)
Maram Habibah	Marc (Cram)
Hannah	Emit (Time)
Ivan Navi	Nori (Iron)
Elle	Selah (Hales)
Viv	Pilut (Tulip)
Savas	Trevoc (Covert)
Anina	Bard (Drab)
Bob	Dennis (Sinned)
Asa	Levart (Travel)
Itati	Mood (Doom)
Nan	Reeb (Beer)
Gereg	Elbissop (Possible)
Kilik	Burg (Grub)
Ailia	Ergo (Ogre)
Nolon	
Siris	
Otto	

*The only *EXCEPTION* to this rule is Doe. Doe is the designated last name used for unidentified persons, whether living or dead; plus, my brain pooped out of ideas.

Credits

All quotations of *Walden* are credited to the original work:

Thoreau, Henry David. *Walden; Or, Life in the Woods*. Boston: Ticknor and Fields, 1854.

Acknowledgements

I know it is standard procedure for athletes and actors to thank God for an award or accomplishment. I won't judge the validity of their thankfulness or their belief in God. I hope you won't judge mine as well.

Thank you, Lord, for this opportunity. I wasn't sure at first if this journey was part of Your will but once I started writing, I knew this is exactly what You wanted for me. I would not, and could not, have created this book without Your guidance and wisdom. I hope this work will be an example of Philippians 4:13 and the unlimited things You can accomplish in a limited, sinful being.

I want to thank my husband, Garrett, for his incredible support through this whole process. I came to you one night and told you I wanted to join a paid writing group so I could possibly write and publish a book and you told me to go for it. You encouraged me through the multiple rounds of drafting and editing and sacrificed to help fund this book to fruition. I appreciate your love and support. I love you more than the stars in the sky and I can't wait for you to read my first book!

Thank you to my sweet dog, Cloud, for always being glued to

my side early in the morning, late at night, and on the weekends as I pumped out this story. You can't read or use thumbs to open this book but I can imagine it'll be an exciting day for our little family when this book is published. I can guarantee ice cream in our celebration.

I want to recognize my "kids" for inspiring me to write this book. Whether you were a former student from CCA, a student-teaching student from MV, or a student at FJH (past, current, or future), YOU were the reason I wrote this book and I hope you know you can do anything you want if you **work hard** at it.

I'd like to thank my family (blood, in-law, and out-law) for their support and encouragement in this adventure in fiction. I'd name all of you but that would take a few pages.

My book wouldn't be nearly as cool without the cover art by Paper & Sage Design. I appreciate Chris answering all my random questions and Christa capturing my vision and aesthetic. The cover is gorgeous and I'm so happy with it.

Thank you to my editors D. Tinker and L.A. Boles. This story was mediocre until you two got your beautiful, creative hands on it.

I am so thankful for my alpha readers Kristine Haecker and Kali Moulton for their delightful notes (and drawings) at a time in the process when I really needed an attagirl.

My beta readers were so important to me and this book. Thank you to Gaston Fox, Gabrielle Damerow, Carla Redinger, Samantha Thomas, and William Dando for your encouraging notes and young adult insight to help make this story realistic and entertaining.

A huge thanks goes out to my glitter sisters from my Facebook writing groups, Creative Central Fictionpreneuers and Fiction Expedition Masters. Debbie Burns, head unicorn, I never would've written this book if you hadn't talked me out of abandoning it. Thank you for your wisdom, tools, and love throughout this process. I also want to thank my FE sisters, original and new, for their tips and critiques on my many #help posts. I want to name all of you individually but that would also take an entire page. You know who you are!! #glittercannon I did it!

A special thanks to my #soulsisters Christina Osborne and Lenore Boles for their blunt, sassy, loving, and helpful guidance. It was meant to be that we ended up on the same journey together and I couldn't be more grateful for that.

Thank you to my best friends Sarah Coffey and Danielle Buck for encouraging me to write my dreams down because they would "make a good book" and for loving YA fiction as much as I do. Sorry Sarah, #TeamPeeta forever.

To the ones I forgot or to my future fans: Thanks, and I love you too!

About the Author

Emily Van Engen tells people often and proudly: "Middle schoolers are my people." Teenagers in general, with their awkwardness and angst, are exactly the room of people she wants to get trapped in. [Well maybe not trapped unless there is an abundant supply of snacks and deodorant.] She writes YA fiction to show her students that they can achieve anything if they work hard, and she plans to continue writing and teaching until she's so old the school forces her into retirement. Though she spent most of her life as a proud Virginian, Van Engen now happily embraces her life as a Michigander, including the three seasons of winter. When she isn't teaching her "kids" at school or writing about the ones that occupy her mind, she's at home reading or being lazy with her husband and dog, Cloud, who you can follow on Instagram: @cloudpups (he's quite popular). Her YA speculative fiction short story, *Paranormal Polka Dots,* will be featured in an anthology called *Winter Whimsy* in November 2018.

For more books and updates:
www.emilyvanengen.com
whatsup@emilyvanengen.com
Instagram: @emilyvanengen

*In case you are wondering, she pronounces her last name Van (like one you drive) Engen (rhymes with vegan but without the V, or the diet).